Poacher's
Faith

Poacher's Faith

MARC SÉGUIN

Translated by
Kathryn Gabinet-Kroo

Library and Archives Canada Cataloguing in Publication

Séguin, Marc, 1970-
[Foi du braconnier. English]
    Poacher's faith : a novel / Marc Séguin ; Kathryn Gabinet-Kroo

Translation of: La foi du braconnier.
ISBN 978-1-55096-314-4

    I. Gabinet-Kroo, Kathryn, 1953- II. Title. III. Title: Foi du braconnier. English.

PS8637.E476F6413 2013   C843'.6   C2013-900141-7

Design and Composition by Mishi Oroboros
Typeset in Birka and American Typewriter at the Moons of Jupiter Studios
Cover: "I love America and America loves me pt.1" by Mark Séguin, 2008

Published by Exile Editions Ltd ~ www.ExileEditions.com
144483 Southgate Road 14 – GD, Holstein, Ontario, N0G 2A0
Printed and Bound in Canada in 2013 by Imprimerie Gauvin

We acknowledge the financial support of the Government of Canada through the
National Translation Program for Book Publishing for our translation activities. We
would also like to acknowledge the Canada Council for the Arts, the Government of
Canada through the Canada Book Fund (CBF), the Ontario Arts Council, and the
Ontario Media Development Corporation, for our overall publishing activities.

Conseil des Arts Canada Council
du Canada   for the Arts

ONTARIO ARTS COUNCIL
CONSEIL DES ARTS DE L'ONTARIO
50 YEARS OF ONTARIO GOVERNMENT SUPPORT OF THE ARTS
50 ANS DE SOUTIEN DU GOUVERNEMENT DE L'ONTARIO AUX ARTS

 Canada

 Ontario
Ontario Media Development
Corporation

Canadian Sales: The Canadian Manda Group, 165 Dufferin Street,
Toronto ON M6K 3H6   www.mandagroup.com   416 516 0911

North American and international Distribution, and U.S. Sales:
Independent Publishers Group, 814 North Franklin Street,
Chicago IL 60610   www.ipgbook.com   toll free: 1 800 888 4741

to Emma

The next morning, I wasn't dead. I woke up, as usual. Emma had gone to drive the little one to daycare.

I went out to shop for the restaurant. The public market. Christmas music. Seasonal vegetables, a bit of fruit. The last, greying apples of the year. Russets, the ones that you can cook without turning them to mush. I had been thinking about adding rabbit stuffed with apples and foie gras to the menu. The stalls still offered fresh produce, even in December: potatoes, salsify, Jerusalem artichokes. Vegetables planted in May and bought on a snow-covered sidewalk in the dead of winter. During the year, it will go from minus thirty to plus thirty degrees Celsius. My arms were weighed down by ten bags, each one hooked onto a finger. My winter coat was too warm. Sweat ran lazily down my back, following the hollow of my spine until it reached the elastic band of my boxers. I walked normally, keeping mostly to myself, not looking at anyone and trying to avoid eye contact. Eyes straight ahead but looking beyond what was in front of me. I assumed that people were aware of this because I am fairly good at being withdrawn. I don't want polite greetings or the smiles of strangers. I generally detest the people I don't know and hate the ones I do.

I was never the kind of guy who quickly understood important situations; I always misunderstood the things that are essential, things to do with love. It took me a few seconds or minutes, sometimes hours or even days to arrange the words I heard in an order that made sense. Emma's words.

I was just getting back to the car when I finally figured out what she wanted to tell me last night when I climbed into bed. Bang. Blackout. Power failure. Everything shuts down and it takes me a second or two to comprehend what is going on right in front of my eyes and inside my head. A prayer is a private thought that no one else can hear. I swore silently to myself but perhaps also out loud. I don't really know because all I could hear was the siren going off inside my skull. A sort of tinnitus of the mind. Out of sync. Time wasn't passing swiftly enough. Over the market's loudspeakers, Dean Martin crooned a saccharine-sweet Christmas tune about a wintry marshmallow world.

I reviewed the past week. The caribou I hadn't killed. My return from the North. Monsignor Vecellio – Pietro – who had died in November. I thought about Emma and all the years that had led me to her, today.

I went back over last night without emotion, disembodied, as if someone else were describing it.

I sat in the car and looked at a worn-out roadmap of North America, taken – torn, to be honest – from an atlas. Across the page, a febrile hand had written FUCK YOU in blue ink and squared-off capital letters. It was my handwriting.

It was over. The odometer set back to zero. I looked up into the rear-view mirror.

The motor was not running.

"*Sata' Karite Ken?*" How are you?
"*Wakata' Karite.*" Fine.

No.

I thought I had pulled the trigger, but I didn't
hear the gunshot. The trigger was gold-plated. I remember
having felt a heaviness, a contorted fall and a dull sound. No
pain. I didn't feel myself dying. Yet I had imagined this scene
as a horror show with blood, bone and brains splattered over
ceilings, walls and floors. And if I'd had a glass eye, they would
have found it intact, fifteen feet away from my head. End of
story. I don't recall any ambient noise. A silent film. The gun's
cold barrel in my wide open mouth and a long descent
through the air's gentle resistance. The ground rising up.

I went back over the ritual and the precise movements, no
faltering, and I saw the gun turn toward my head – the Italian
rifle that I've used for hunting for the past ten years – and I
remembered that the French call a gun's bore, the part
through which the bullet passes, *l'âme*. The soul.

I got up. My eyes heavy, the taste of black truffle in my
mouth. Could death taste like truffles, I wondered. Then I felt
a huge relief at having managed to die. One shotgun shell for
less than a dollar. And very little moral or emotional cost, if
any, resulting in roughly the same symptoms as an interview
or an airplane landing in turbulence: butterflies in the stomach, dizziness and cold, clammy hands. Can Death be a destination? Like going on vacation? Like a sign along the highway
welcoming you to town? That's it, you're here. It's always so
important to know where you are.

I was standing, but off-balance, almost drunk. I went over
to the window and saw cars, the same anonymous cars as

always, the same buses entering and exiting the municipal garage. Still no noise. Or maybe just an uninspired soundtrack coming from the TV. It seemed to me that the passers-by had changed and were now even more indifferent than they'd been the day before. I wanted to float or see a light or find myself in total darkness. It wasn't like that, wherever I was. The sidewalks were still grey but snow had begun to fall. As ironic as it may seem, I didn't want to be disappointed, but no sooner said than done... This was not at all how I had envisioned my demise. I turned away from the window to see if what they say is true: that you could see your body remaining, so to speak, among the living. Nope. It was still evening and I was still inside myself. One day, I'd like to feel that my intellect is somewhere other than behind my eyes.

Obviously I wasn't dead.

I had probably fainted before the bullet left the gun. Excitement or fear. I told myself I'd have to add a postscript to my letter to say that I wasn't dead. I also remember telling myself that this was quite an odd experience. I didn't know it yet, but I would never again feel the need to kill myself. Emma would cure me of that.

I removed the piece of paper that I had put into a white Hilroy envelope. Mouth too dry to lick the seal, I had tucked the flap inside, as if I were going to hand-deliver it. Besides, handling someone else's saliva, that transmitter of viruses and other microbes, is disgusting. I prefer self-sealing envelopes. I reread my note.

I retrieved the gun from where it had fallen. A gun lying on the floor is completely inconsistent with normal life: a gun is either stored in a locked cupboard or case where no one sees it or it's in the hands of someone threatening to use it to kill. Guns don't kill without a human's consent. I looked at it for a few more seconds, telling myself that a gun is such an innocuous object once you understand it. It's not as if you want to give it a big hug or anything, but you feel so much less alone when you're armed. Sometimes it even looks like the head of your beloved when she's lying on her stomach. A gun makes you feel strong, like when you're in love. There was still spit on the end of the barrel.

I refolded and pocketed the letter I had written on the end-paper of my old atlas of North America. I unloaded the gun before putting it back into the locked cabinet.

I had just returned from hunting caribou. My duffle bag was still lying on top of the shoes and boots by the front door, right where I had left it when I came back from the Far North. The house was silent. I went upstairs. My family was sleeping.

Elmyna was on her back, her arms flung above her head. Perfectly serene. The blanket rose and fell with her every breath. I had to smile as I backed out of her room.

I went to our room and slid under the covers, gently and carefully, almost guiltily, like a guy who'd gotten drunk and was coming home late.

I pressed my lips to the nape of Emma's warm neck. I love a woman's neck.

She wasn't asleep.

She turned to me, gave me a long kiss and whispered something in my ear.

Emma, whom I loved like a prayer that would be answered.

October 1991.

I only learned about it four days later at a Holiday Inn in Winnipeg. The black bear that I had killed in Manitoba's Riding Mountain National Park weighed more than 350 kilos. The headline of a little news item on the right-hand page of the *Globe and Mail* read "Monster Shot Down by Poacher."

I knew the animal was huge as soon as I saw the thick black bulk of its body appear on the road. I was glad to see no one ahead of me and no one in my rear-view mirror. I don't seek these things out, but they do happen to me, just like some people happen to read and love Proust and others happen to play the violin, or write, or learn a new language, I guess. It's a talent or some kind of predisposition whose codes are still a mystery to me.

By locking the wheels with a calculated twist of the steering wheel, I slued the back of the pickup across the road in just the right way. In a split second, I was able to open my door with my left hand while with my right, I grabbed the gun lying on the floor in front of the passenger seat. The bear had stopped, curious like almost all wild animals – too curious. Bang. Gunned down on the spot.

I am a consequence of modern America, the America that gunpowder conquered and made a conqueror. Even if I am an intellectual product of the middle class, one half white and the other half American Indian. Still flowing through my veins are the motives of a predator. Or a "regulator," as the biologists and hunters aware of hunting's bad reputation would say. It should be called "Removing the resource." Bunch of hypocrites. I kill animals so I don't kill men. Gives men a bit of a reprieve. When I can, I bring back part of the animal to eat and I make no effort to hide the body. A ton of other species in the food chain can make use of the carcass.

At best, I would get the bear out of plain sight, but that would only be to delay discovery of my misdeed. No question of bringing the whole thing back: it would be impossible to move. I don't think I could even have lifted it the metre necessary to hoist it into the bed of the pickup. That settled it. Had it been a human, I would have had to camouflage the body because the root of that problem is frankly quite simple: no body, no crime. But here again, the weight was a burden. That is why killers, in the controlled perpetration of the act, carve up their victims. They're thinking ahead.

The *Globe and Mail* said that, of course, the bear's gallbladder was missing. No kidding. Someone paid me forty-five hundred dollars for that one gallbladder. In 1991, that was an incredible amount of money for an Institut d'hôtellerie cooking student. The bile alone is worth up to twenty times its weight in gold if you know how to prepare it. The recipe calls for the organ, which looks like a long dried-up crabapple, to be dried in total darkness, cut into three or four pieces and then marinated in several bottles of whiskey or scotch. "Seems it'll cure what ails you, eh, my friend?" I had said out loud. I always talk to the animal I've just killed: it does help personalize the relationship of dominance.

A cold? Try a hot toddy made with bear-bile scotch. Erectile dysfunction? A shot of bear whiskey. The following year, in 1992, the American black bear would be added to the list of animals named in CITES, an agreement that prohibits the sale of organs removed from threatened or endangered species.

Asian prescriptions abound. But death? No one knows if that will cure what ails us. Not even the Chinese, and there are many more of them dying than there are of us.

As for the bear in Manitoba, he died dead in his tracks. If I had to calculate where it happened, the exact location of the stretch of dirt road that ran through Riding Mountain National Park, I would say that it lay on the imaginary yellow line. "Bullet to the brain," I'd whispered. Hit squarely in the head, a centimetre below the left ear. Even if animals had the ability to comprehend, he still would never have known he'd died. There was a neat little hole the size of a pea, almost invisible where it had entered, and a sticky red-black crater the size of an apple where it had exited. Eyes wide open. That's how you know when an animal is dead. A human too, I suppose. Eyes closed, it's still alive and you have to finish it off. Open eyes always add a little something extra, a knowing wink when you understand that you are right.

Big wet snowflakes, damp twilight. Loud music: Nirvana's *Nevermind*. The war in Kuwait and Iraq had been over for several months, but the oil-well fires still burned each night on the news. I always loved filling up my tank and smelling the fresh odour of the gas. I could even close my eyes, like you do in a Pepsi challenge, and tell the difference between regular and super. I guess they'd call me a gasophile. "Smells Like Teen Spirit." The band had just released its second album and I listened to it in an endless loop, thanks to the replay button on the cassette player I'd stolen from a car parked on the former Dorchester Boulevard, a street whose name had been changed to Boulevard René-Lévesque in 1987 although Westmount refused to comply. I had taken it from a sky-blue Audi 5000 right in the middle of rush hour and no one had been the least bit surprised. Audi 5000s were so easy, with their little code that served as a key. You had to punch the numbers in to unlock it, but if you held down both the one and the five for eight seconds, you could open the door. One, two, three and the car was mine. Then all I had to do was slide the fingers of one hand behind the audio unit and push it gently toward me.

I had managed to flip the bear onto its back by pulling it to the edge of the ditch with the pickup. The two left paws were still attached to the bumper. I wondered how novelist Jean-Yves Soucy could have imagined the trapper-hero of *Creatures of the Chase* making love to a dead mother bear.

Twisted. Had I been so inclined, I could easily have fucked my bear in the ass, considering how I had him tied up. But that shapeless mass aroused no desire.

You have to start cutting at the solar plexus. There is less fur on the belly, which my Buck 119 knife slit with precision. I am always surprised to find a real warmth inhabiting everything from the stones to the treetops there in the natural, perpetual chill of an October forest. The heat, dying. Life is hot and the bear's slipped away in a cloud of steam. In physics, they say that sublimation is when a solid becomes a gas. I like to know the proper terms for things. In any case, my frozen hands were grateful for this small fortune of blood and steaming organs, which felt almost burning hot in contrast to my icy fingers. Once the bear's skin has been slit to the genitals, which the knife must carefully skirt all the way to the anus, you have to cut the membrane containing the entire paunch and remove it completely to reach the liver. A beautiful web of lace, once used to make sausages and blood pudding.

A 350 kilo animal must have at least 50 kilos of stomach and intestine. It slips and slides and always has the same smell of hot blood: a metallic odour, not at all like perfume or flirtatiousness or baking. There were sucking noises like those you hear when making love, mixed with the sound of my breath, which I held and then released as I turned my head away.

At night, in my bed, when I was little, I tried to break records by holding my breath as long as I could: forty, fifty, sixty seconds. I once held it for over a minute. My stopwatch already registered 104 seconds. I exploded and caught my breath again, completely satisfied and fully convinced that I had won a battle against an imaginary enemy.

I managed to extract from the bear the soft, formless mass of the liver, which suddenly escaped from the belly and slid onto the ground. It was attached to the stomach and I remember smiling when I saw the little cream-coloured mound of the gallbladder attached to the liver. It was the size of a summer apple. I felt like preparing a bear stew with apples and peas.

A dark green vehicle marked with dirty white letters spelling out 'Riding Mountain Manitoba National Park' came toward me from the opposite direction and pulled up next to my truck as I was about to leave.

"Y'all right?" asked a hugely overweight guy in his late thirties or early forties as he turned a knob to lower the volume of a country singer's twangy voice. I would have been very surprised if this park warden had deigned to get out of his vehicle, so I left my blood-stained hands on my knees and nodded that, yes, everything was fine. I explained that I had just stopped to engage the pickup's four drive wheels – in those days, you had to turn a key on the front wheels to switch to four-wheel drive. Our two motors idled slowly. Satisfied with my response, he released his brake and calmly drove off. The sound of his tires on the dirt road was then cloaked by the noise of the motor revving up again. He hadn't noticed the dark carcass barely hidden behind my rear fender. It's crazy how fear and nervousness can go undetected if you seem normal and calm. Or almost. He had, however, noticed that I had a Quebec licence plate. A little later, the park authorities would figure out that I was one of their suspects. The same obese warden would be the one to discover the slaughtered bear in that very spot the next morning, but I would already have crossed the border by then. After doing a search for the colour and make of my truck, my name would turn up on a list of probable suspects. But with no concrete proof, they couldn't make any accusations. From then on, I would be registered with TRAFFIC, a policing organization, a kind of biological Interpol that monitors the trafficking of animal organs and plants. Suspected poacher.

ON THE FLY
A blue two-ton 1987 Dakota pickup truck with Quebec plates travels down a rough road in Manitoba's Riding Mountain National Park. Night is falling. In this protected park's dense forest, a male bear lumbers along and enters an opening. The falling snow has covered the ground and disguised the odours, making prey harder to track. The bear hesitates upon seeing this open area, which resembles a clearing. In the middle of this glade of rocks and sand, two shining fires burn to his left. A muffled sound, but just as luminous, rings out and the bear is struck down by a violent, burning blow. A man comes out, and busies himself with the dead animal for a few minutes. Later, a man driving a green pickup approaches the blue Dakota from the opposite direction. The two trucks remain still for several minutes before each continues on its own way.

I drove all night, changing provinces and heading west to Esterhazy, Saskatchewan. From there I went south to cross into the U.S. at North Portal and on to Stanley, a little hick town in North Dakota. A billboard read 'Welcome to Stanley, Population: 1371, Families: 678.'

North Portal is a miniscule border crossing with one lone customs agent per shift. The building would have resembled a private home if it weren't for the steel fences that you could only pass through once the light turned green. Ten metres beyond it, a sign read 'Welcome to Portal, USA.' You lower your window and wait, in good faith it seemed to me, since it certainly took at least five minutes before a human form appeared. I had been thinking about public bathrooms or, to be more precise, about how men's urinals are such filthy things and how every time a man takes a leak, some falls on the floor and other men step in it and then they also piss droplets onto the floor, and how all these strange men's pee can end up on the soles of my shoes, on my floor and on the carpeting in my pickup, thus creating an extraordinarily well-travelled pee soup.

"Yep," said the woman six times too heavy for her height. I always thought North Americans were thinner than everyone else in the world.

"I'm going to Stanley on a hunting trip."

Everything was normal. North Dakota is an immense hunting ground, and aside from the semi-trailers, hunters made up the principal clientele at this border crossing. The gallbladder was cooling on a block of ice, next to a wild-mushroom sandwich and a can of beer. I would have been surprised if the customs lady had known what a bear's gallbladder looked like, but in that case I would have told her it was an edible piece of meat. Then I could have taken a bite of it as proof and become immortal.

"Okay, go."

In Stanley, I packed the gallbladder on ice and shipped it off to Montreal, to the Republic of Szechuan Restaurant on La Gauchetière. Twenty-four hours. The FedEx employee wrote 'gift' on the package, so that there'd be less chance of an inspection at the border, and I gave the name of the Minister of Natural Resources and Wildlife as the sender, using the actual address of the only motel in Stanley, though I would never even set foot inside one of its rooms.

I went back through the border at Portal. This time the Canadian customs officer decided to mess with me, asking routine questions along with a few about animal psychology.

"Where do you live?"

"Montreal."

"That's a long ways away. Purpose of the trip?"

"Hunting, *la chasse*," I answered, knowing full well that adding the French would stir up trouble for me because in this country, the most bilingual in the world, unilingual people always feel threatened.

"Any cigarettes or alcohol?" he asked through tight lips.

"No, sir, went hunting and didn't have time to go to the liquor store, and whatever I had, I drank it all back there."

"How many bottles do you have?"

"None, sir."

"Tobacco products?"

"No."

I can always tell when my blood pressure goes up. My ears get red. And then my mouth goes dry and my head feels all hot inside. I don't get angry at customs officers who do their job, only at the ones who go overboard, acting as if you should take them for idiots.

"Are you carrying any firearms?"

"Motherfucking asshole!" I said to myself. No, I go hunting with a baseball bat!

"Yes."

I didn't want to answer "yes, sir" because that would be insolent and he'd know it.

"I have a Winchester 30-30, model 94. And a state permit for big game, too. Wanna see it?"

He responded with only a shake of his head because Canadian Customs could not care less about an American hunting license, which I didn't have anyway.

"Can I see some ID?" he asked, turning his head and looking at me for what seemed to me like the first time.

Average man, average human. Anonymous like the majority of the hundred billion humans who've been born up until now. I already knew what I was looking for when I reached into my pocket for the little packet of cards held together by a rubber band. One by one, I sifted through my credit card, student ID, bank card, driver's license, social insurance card… until I finally came to the blue one with my picture in the left-hand corner under the heading 'Communauté Mohawk Community, Canada.' He took it and read my name: Marc S. Morris.

"Welcome to Canada," he said, handing back the card without looking at me again, no smile, no anger. Case dismissed.

I retraced my steps, taking the 9 to Kennedy, Saskatchewan and heading due east toward Manitoba. Wawota, Elkhorn, Rivers, Rapid City and Brandon to the south.

We made love that first night and she kept her
eyes open. My goose was cooked. I realize this only now. The
order of things is totally messed up, even if it all makes sense
in the end. That's the driving force behind our universe and
our horoscopes: anticipation is a volition as powerful as its
realization and its realization will always be applied to its
anticipation. So, provided we simply refer to it, we will always
find self-validation there.

You cannot look a woman in the eyes when you're making
love unless you intend to meet her parents.

A little hotel in Brandon. I hadn't been looking for her.
A single mother with a seven-year-old daughter. She herself
was the daughter of a French-speaking single mother and,
like her mother, she had been abandoned by her husband
when he learned she was pregnant. She was a forestry engineer forced to take a leave of absence because her daughter
had come down with roseola. Under normal circumstances,
she would have been the one who met me on the road in
Riding Mountain National Park just when that bear
ambled across my path two days earlier. There are coincidences you just can't make up but which are still quite un-
believable.

She was twenty-seven; I was twenty-one. Her name was
Nelly. She had already been to Montreal. Relationships exist
simply because destiny, or whatever it is that we don't ascer-
tain directly from life, reveals itself. We met at the gas station

27

first. Two looks and a mutual understanding. Then we saw each other again at the local restaurant. She was a pretty girl. Lean and lanky but with a great figure, angular yet shapely. I was sure her breasts weren't real, even though I'd never touched them. In 1991, the chances of running into a lady engineer with breast implants 150 kilometres west of Winnipeg must have been pretty slim. I was disappointed, by reason of my anthropological curiosity.

We spent one night, one day and part of another night together. After those thirty hours, I think I came within a hair's breadth of marrying her, but she'll never know it because I cavalierly took off when I felt she was looking a little too far into the future. Or maybe it was me. I had begun to detest what the human race expected of me; I hated predictable things like love, family and the social roles that are imposed on us. Obviously, I had also kept my eyes open. It's beautiful to look at each other that way, to believe in something bigger, to believe that if you're looking into each other's eyes, it will be more sincere, more authentic. And yet the biggest crooks I've ever known can look you straight in the eye. Eyes that avoid making contact always tell more truths than those that meet you head-on.

That second time I saw her we were at the local diner in Brandon. She was in the bathroom. I thought maybe I'd gone into the wrong one, but she was using the men's room because her daughter Megan was in the lady's. Women always pee at the same time. I pushed on the door and she said, "Busy!" I was surprised and apologized in French: "*Désolé!*" The voice behind the door responded in kind, "*Pas de quoi.*" No problem.

I stood outside the door, listening to her urinate. Stealing a little bit of her privacy. Smile and a smile in return. "The seat's warm," she said without looking at me as she went to join her daughter, who was already putting on her coat. She had left the seat covered with toilet paper, in a very feminine attempt at hygiene.

I had ordered fish and chips, the special of the day. It was revolting: in oil that was almost rancid, they had cooked potatoes of dubious quality and a cod that had been shipped to the middle of the continent at some unknown time and in a questionable manner.

As she was leaving, she threw me a line.

"You must be here for the hunting," she said, pointing to my pickup.

"Among other things," I replied.

"Do you have a license for hunting the female of the species?"

I couldn't think of an answer. I thought of the other meaning, which had to be on her mind as well. I was still looking for words when this flash of lightning took us by surprise. No words. I had understood. I guess it was a trick question. If I said I didn't hunt females, she would understand my refusal and if I said I did, I would sound like a total incompetent: four-legged females are very easy to find and that would make

29

me a piss-poor hunter. I smiled and lowered my eyes, and that said it all.

The first time around, we didn't come. Neither one of us. Out of respect? Embarrassment? Clumsiness or anxiety? Thinking back on it, I believe she could have managed it, since at one point she had whispered, "I wanna climb on you." I don't know why, but she never did "climb." It didn't immediately click in my mind that she could come by straddling me. Chalk it up to inexperience. And without further ado, our arousal levelled off until the mechanics came to an end. Later I would learn that being "ridden" by a woman who wants to come is a privilege, and it arouses not only the lover and husband in me, but also the voyeur and the porn-film actor. This distance that is so dear to men and so lacking in women.

I remembered a line from Shakespeare's heroine in *Two Gentlemen of Verona*: "Since maids, in modesty, say 'no' to that which they would have the profferer construe 'ay.'" No means yes: the basic rationale presented by rapist and romantic hero alike.

Our shadows were cast by the light of the moon. We were on her bed. I was lying down, she was sitting with her chin resting on her knees, which she had tucked up against her chest. She said, in suddenly hesitant French, that this was the first time she had ever slept with a man she'd just met. On that night in October 1991, I became a man for someone. She had said "man." Twenty-one years old and for the first time, I felt the giddiness of an adult. I had to laugh to cover up the extent to which her comment had filled me with equal doses of fear and euphoria. I would never have guessed that she intended to make love had she not invited me to her place to have coffee and "talk a bit." I regret not having read Shakespeare earlier.

Nelly. I didn't know what to say when I left her.

Yekathsnenhtha'. Descending.

Ke'entie. Toward the south.

I got back on the road going south. Toward the bottom of the map in my Philip's Atlas. A straight line to the middle of North Dakota, again. I went back over the border at an open checkpoint. No town on either side. Only a sign: Entering the United States of America, Land of the Free. And then all the regulations to be respected if you're carrying drugs, firearms or endangered species: report to the appropriate authorities if you think you are breaking the law. Obviously.

I called my mother from a telephone booth when I went to fill up my tank. She thought I was in Montreal and asked nothing about where I was.

"*Ohnensto enioshen'ne o'harasheha.*" Have some corn chowder tomorrow night?

"I can't, not tomorrow...yeah...I'll call when I get in."

I adore corn chowder, but I prefer salmon-head soup.

South. Dunseith – Rugby – Harvey, all the way to Steele. On the odometer: 341 kilometres. Eighty-six degrees to the east. Jamestown to Fargo. And another 340 kilometres to the north and Canadian Customs at Pembina. Recipe note: supreme of wild goose, meat glaze and mooseberries. Arrival in Winnipeg, Canada. I thought about Nelly as I drove the 1,675 kilometres of this U.

We saw each other again in Winnipeg. I called her when I arrived, from a Holiday Inn on the highway. The planes flew over my head. Without waiting. She was taking two more days. Brandon is ninety minutes from Winnipeg.

"Wanna come to Brandon?" she asked first.

"Sorry, I can't retrace my steps," I answered in French. "I'll tell you all about it."

And so we made love again for two straight days, going out only to get a bite to eat and to buy condoms. Each time I entered her, she said, "Gotta put your raincoat on." Calm, everything under control. She had this "click" that only certain women possess: you go as far in as possible, and then when you give a little extra push, you feel like you've gone a centimetre deeper. It makes kind of a "click."

It gave me a funny feeling of warmth just above the bone because, since she came when she straddled me, it ended up leaving traces. I couldn't control myself one second more. She liked that we came together. I guess it was romantic. I hated it.

On the first morning, we were still in bed when we heard the sound of the newspaper being tossed on the doorstep. She got up, wearing just an old tee shirt and panties. It was the first time I had seen her from the back. Erection. She wanted to read. I, on the other hand, wanted to enter her with all my might. Plow right through her.

"Fucking jerks," she sighed through her teeth.

"What?" I asked, mechanically because I had a rising tide of blood flooding the middle of my body. I had definitely heard the plural "jerkssssss," even though I knew I'd done nothing wrong. But when you're a man born in the twentieth century, guilt is always part of any relationship with any woman. Like an electronic chip installed in the factory. I had my hand on my penis. Low tide in my head.

And that's when I learned that my bear weighed 350 kilos. That's also when I learned that we should have met on that forest path, four days earlier.

Back in the car. "Come on, Nel. We'll let the dust settle and we'll talk again." Her eyes were full of tears when I closed the door. A little more and she'd have asked me if this was love.

ON THE FLY

A blue, two-ton Dakota pickup crosses the border four times, with no clear destination. Four days later, the vehicle's trajectory, from Riding Mountain Park to Winnipeg, forms a group of lines that are visually recognizable and understandable as part of a Western alphabet. The first letter is an F and the second is a U. 1,790 kilometres.

My Mohawk mother officially made me an American Indian. A ghost of the past. It's a title that I use only on very rare occasions because technically, since my mother left the reservation to marry a White, my Indian blood will dry up with me. No such privilege for my offspring, unless I go back to live on the reserve. Never. The most accurate reality of our identity would be described as the blood of a dying society that is quietly imploding while the world turns a blind eye. They've hidden our demise in suburban basements. Behind two TVs, sofas, garage doors, playpens and shopping centres with parking lots. Millions of parking spaces. Asphalt is an illusion of progress. *Tekatkennyer.* Defeat.

In the summer of 1990, I was among those who closed traffic on the Mercier Bridge to this white suburban America. I joined a handful of American Warriors who didn't really understand why they were wearing masks and carrying assault rifles on a bridge spanning the Saint Lawrence to defend a cause that appeared just. The Mohawk community is Iroquois. Historically, the Iroquois were bloodthirsty Indians at war with the other tribes, mainly Algonquins. It wasn't this red blood that made me aware of my true nature; rather it was having understood that human nature is built on a vague morality that is totally separate from common sense. A man's public rebellion always hides private reasons, the real ones.

I didn't take up arms because of a golf club or the violation of an ancient Mohawk burial ground, but because of my hatred for this continent and its capitalist values, its religious hypocrisy and its overconsumption.

I treasure a photo from the *New York Times* that shows me holding a sign bearing a message written in red: *Aiontakia 'tohtahrho*. Alienate someone. America seduced itself with guns and ever since this incestuous victory, it has not stopped its self-promotion. I was born in 1970, in the fall of the 10,000 day war. I am more American than an American. I grew up with weapons in my hands, in my mouth, in my eyes – I'm a natural-born killer.

A deeply hidden desire for conquest is beginning to boil over inside me. An urge to dominate. But this new awareness will cause earthquakes: two tectonic plates resting one on top of the other. Forty degrees Celsius of revolt. And the shaking takes different, sometimes worrying forms. I was led to believe that the individual is greater than his mass. That the salvation of the soul is obtained only through the pursuit of happiness. I hate the idea of happiness. They say that the human brain runs on sugar. Happiness is an artificial sweetener. A substitute.

They want to violate my genetic makeup. America is a virus. I am a chill. Fever is a rebellion.

I was going to start cooking classes at the Institut d'hôtellerie in the fall. It was my clear intention to become a famous chef and make a lot of money. At the time, careers in modeling were all the rage. Fashion was in fashion. Girls were getting thinner. While real life was growing fat behind the scenes, anorexia was parading itself across the front page. Little girls dressed up like women. You saw them everywhere, raised to the level of stardom by an appearance-based society. I masturbated in front of a poster of Claudia Schiffer. It took me a year to realize that life is easy: making money is easy, bedding women is easy, wanting to be an all-around good guy is hardly complicated, lying is an art, and "impersonating" life was far too simple. I felt giddy. I sought out taboos, no sooner found than broken. I excelled at school. The rebels and underground types all ended up mainstream, except for two or three punk bands hanging out in Brooklyn basements. Hope, too. This new continent of pavement and parking lots was a disappointment. I resented it. Blasé at twenty-one. I decided to take charge of things. As long as I was allowing myself to self-destruct, I was going to help and participate in the process.

Explosion is spectacular. Implosion is more devastating because you don't see it. Like cancer.

Our most serious crime may still be killing another man, but considering the positive publicity surrounding these criminals, I had my doubts. At the end of my first year in CEGEP, actually at the beginning of my second year, I bought myself a blue and green Philip's Atlas. On page nine you could see our continent, from the southern United States to the

Northwest Territories. I don't know why, but these topographical maps have always fascinated me. I carried this one around in my knapsack. With its millions of places and coordinates, I didn't feel quite so lost. Even nowhere is mapped. This was before Google Earth but after a course on meat. Cutting, cooking, stock, deglazing, demi-glace, glaze, service.

I was sleeping with Denise, a great girl that I would never have married because of her first name. She had told me over Styrofoam cups of coffee that I lacked courage – all that nattering of an eighteen-year-old girl who believed she would start a family, have children and always be in love, even as a widow. There and then, listening to her talk about her needs, or rather about society's needs, my slumbering hatred was awakened. Ask no questions, Denise, and do as the others do, the model's so simple when it's unique. Lack of courage, she'd said. I was afraid, she'd added. I thought I had tripped over my pride, but what suddenly rose up out of the earth was not a question of hormones or hubris, but rather the wooden handle of a hatchet. I dug it out of the ground.

Sometimes the virus wins and makes the brain believe that aspartame is a sugar.

Since I didn't know how to respond to these affirmations, which I now know to have been just, my hands – not knowing what to do either – removed the atlas and a blue pen from my knapsack. As she silently stared at me, accusing and tight-lipped, I calmly drew a gigantic FUCK YOU that began in Saskatchewan and whose final U ended somewhere in the

Saint Lawrence near Montmagny. And I showed it to her as I stood to go. I left and never saw her again. That was the first time I had left someone. I was the bad guy. I kept the atlas.

There is always a fire within. Sometimes it was in love, with a high school girl or a stuffed toy. One time it was the fire of bravado, of opposition, a drag race. Another time, a fire nourished by human hope. Or by the north-south injustice or by society's lies about equality. A million times I thought I'd put it out, but the embers stayed so hot that the slightest breeze brought the flame back to life.

So I read all the books the world had to offer, believing they were fountains to quench my thirst. Proust, Hemingway, the melancholy Russians, García Márquez, Borges, Kundera, Flaubert. Even Maurice Maeterlinck's *Death*: "Death and death alone is what we must consult about life; and not some vague future or survival, in which we shall not be present. It is our own end; and everything happens in the interval between death and now."

Aside from a few of them, books are mirages.

The second god I loved was the interlude. The first one that I loved voluntarily. I believed in time. That everything in the world came only as a result of time. I love you, you love me...time will tell. Seems that time takes care of everything. From point A to point B. Time is the space that separates everything from the truth.

It took me three days to trace the C and the K of FUCK. In the end, only a good part of the K was completed because I stopped in Chicago before finishing it. I don't think it's too serious. One of the two best fresh fish markets on the entire continent is in Chicago. I never understood that. Maybe because of a heightened demand. New York, Chicago and Japan are the only places to get fresh fish. Any other place would have, at best, twelve hours less freshness, which is to say there's a world of difference.

I was hired as a cook's helper in a Japanese restaurant called Sea. Only one full day and I had a real job. I'd pretended that I already had my diploma. This was before there was a sushi bar on every corner. Sea's walls were actually giant aquariums where you could watch your next meal swimming. Seeing your food still alive would be quite chic in hip restaurants five years later. At first, half the population found this idea disgusting, but since things tend to work out for the best, those people stayed away from the place while the others came in droves. The list of reservations and the restaurant were always full. You showed your waiter the fish you wanted and an employee "fished" for it with a net. "This one, sir?" and off he went to the kitchen, holding the wriggling fish in a bowl, one hand under it and one hand on top.

After my shift – actually, there was only one – the kitchen staff made themselves something to eat, as was the custom in better establishments. With little more than a look, I had made a connection with a cook's helper named Eugenia.

Nineteen years old, born in a Detroit suburb to an American mother and a Yugoslavian father who had played hockey for his national hockey team before defecting to the West during a tournament in 1972. She had told me briefly about her background between two emulsions – which had gotten me hired on the spot – and her job at the plating station. As the service wound down and the employees began to prepare their meals, I quickly understood that the kitchen had been infused with a spirit of competition between the candidates and their monstrous chef-to-be egos. The half-Japanese boss was not in the kitchen during this performance. I had asked Eugenia to help me. I had an idea.

Throughout my childhood, I spent weekends with my grandmother on the reservation, and at the end of every April, we went fishing for brown bullhead on the little tributaries of the great Saint Lawrence River. "Seek to enter via the small rivers and not directly via the ocean," wrote Thomas Aquinas about acquiring knowledge, sometime before he became a saint. So off we went on foot with a bamboo rod, a simple hook and a jar of earthworms. Only two requirements: that the sun had melted the ice and that the bottom of the stream or little river was muddy. We sat on the banks and this lazy fish, cousin to the famous catfish, bit every time. An oily fish with red flesh and dark skin. Big head, moustaches and two pointed barbs behind the head that will inject a numbing substance into a careless hand. Such an ugly face that after a few seconds, it becomes beautiful. "The beautiful is ugly," wrote Baudelaire, and he was right. Such flesh! Early in the season, just after the lakes thaw and before they get that muddy taste, it's a very fine fish. The Japanese don't eat catfish – something I hadn't known and would learn soon enough. Instead, they have an ancient and enduring respect for this domesticated fish because its sudden and abnormal agitation in the aquarium invariably announces an earthquake or a tsunami.

Of all the fish I've ever fished for, this one was certainly the most difficult to kill. I remember hours spent sitting on riverbanks, watching out of the corner of my eye as all those mouths tirelessly opened and closed. Seeing them move, opening and closing their mouths to the same slow rhythm, even after having gutted them. "It's their nerves," said my grandmother upon seeing my dumbfounded seven-year-old face observing the scene and trying to comprehend death. As if nerves did not belong to the cycle of life. Will I too have these moments of reprieve once I am dead? Will I still have a few more minutes to speak of death once my life is over?

I plunged the net into the bottom of an aquarium and caught the only catfish that I could see and that, it seemed to me, had escaped the menu and the oven that night. I had been quick and no one paid much attention to the flesh that I was now preparing. Eugenia smiled, ignorant as she also was that the fish had a name.

Besides our meals, the employees also were allowed a beer or a glass of wine. Eugenia was one of those women who, after one glass of wine, lose her two lowest ribs on either side, those just above the hips. The middle of the body arches, the butt sticks out, the breasts jut upward and forward. Sex. Two ribs lost per glass of alcohol.

First, using a Japanese knife from Korin in New York that was worth at least three thousand dollars, I prepared the two filets with surgical precision so as not to touch the intestines. While Eugenia sliced one of the filets into strips of sashimi, I sautéed the other half, which I'd coated with rape seed oil – mistakenly known as canola – and then dredged in aniseeds, sesame seeds and *fleur de sel*. But the best was yet to come. I had placed the rest of the fish – the skeleton, head, spine, bones, intestines and fins – on a bed of crushed ice on a long rectangular plate and covered it all with more crushed ice, taking care to shape it into the general form of the original fish, leaving the head and tail sticking out at either end. Atop this icy construction, Eugenia had laid the pieces of sashimi, sprinkled them with fresh chervil, and served the hot filet as an accompaniment on another plate. And we began to eat. At first, no one said anything, but somehow the news reached the chef. As he approached, passing through a small but fascinated crowd, we were calmly eating the flesh of a fish that was still alive, still opening and closing its mouth in unison with ours. It slowed down about ten minutes later, and the mouth remained open in one final spasm.

She smelled good. She told me later that she didn't wear perfume because she was allergic to the base alcohol from which it is made. I had noticed her as soon as I walked into Sea's kitchen that October night. We always know fairly soon where such things will lead. In nature, most mammals also know very quickly what will come of a chance encounter. And in the majority of cases, the male – a mature male – will try to transmit his genes to as many females as possible. Aside from a few differences, all negligible, we still resemble them. Man distanced himself from the mammalian long ago: at the time religion was invented in a dull dark cave while we were still fur-covered beasts. Or maybe it was when the plastic baby bottle was invented. So the male will approach a female, follow her, breathe in her scent and even talk to her, we assume, in order to measure her receptivity. At the end of this exercise, the female will decide whether or not to give her consent.

Eugenia had given me hers a few minutes after I came in. First with a look held a fraction of a second too long and then, in the kitchen, she had brushed by me twice, once nonchalantly pressing her breast against my right arm as she brought me a plate so that I could put a clementine emulsion on a serving of oyster shooters. Later, a leg grazed mine, again lingering a bit too long. Beginning of an erection due to some unknown pheromones or chemical reactions. Like the opposing particles of an atom, we were quickly charged with an energy that would soon draw each of us to the other.

I had had a few conversations with the kitchen staff before the chef, Bill Shan, noticed that I had grilled the restaurant's mascot. They all knew that this brown bullhead catfish would get me into trouble. Jeff, the sous-chef, had even warned me to be very careful, telling me that Shan could really fly off the handle. I was anticipating a fistfight. When he saw our repast, he asked who was responsible. I answered, "Me." He asked how long the fish had survived. "Long enough for us to eat the filets," I told him.

"You're fired" was all he'd said. Years later, I would discover that it had become a featured dish at a very trendy restaurant in Chicago.

I ended up at her place. We walked three blocks and then entered a beautiful apartment on the third floor of an authentically Victorian brick townhouse, which her salary clearly could not cover. She must have read my mind because she said, "The house belongs to my parents. They live on the ground floor."

She was sitting on a pale sofa. The weather was still nice at the end of that Midwestern October. I remember an open window and the sound of cars. She was wearing brown leather mules. DKNY sandals. I saw the brand because she let them dangle from her toes, first one and then the other, as she crossed and uncrossed her legs. Pink cotton capris and a fitted white silk shirt artfully unbuttoned to afford a look at the beginning of a curve: 34B. Later, I would see the size on the label of a bra left or intentionally forgotten on her bathroom sink. Imagining the colour of the sheets or the thickness of the pillows. Desire is a sweet poison. Even on the tip of the tongue, it's a poison. My eyes weighed her breasts through the silk. If I ever kill a man, it will be to cut off his hand and sew it to his eye.

"So are we gonna sleep together?" Her eyes held mine.

Don't flinch, don't let anything show, think of the North Pole and those seals that people hit over the head before sticking them with a pickaxe so they can make airplane seats from their skins. It was during those long seconds that she fell for me, she said. It would have been pretentious to say yes, and a no would have meant that I didn't want to. I had believed her to be direct, enchanting and bold. Later, she confessed to me how nervous she'd been. And before I began to look like a complete idiot, she had gotten up, pretending she had a cramp in her leg. Freed from its trap before the final pain.

Thank goodness. I'd lost my wings. Someone had to finish me off.

That's when I fell for her. From that point on, you know. You don't yet know what, but you know. Deep in my belly, a locomotive was getting underway. Choo-choo. After a long kiss, lying beneath her, her on top, I had reached behind her to pull her panties out of the way and ran a slow finger over her hot, slippery sex. Our eyes were closed and our mouths had ceased kissing and wordless murmuring escaped our lips. We did our thing to the end. She wrapped her legs around my waist with such force that I felt desired. I had quickly had enough for me and I wanted to warn her that I was going to come – I am a nice guy, after all. I expected a "let go" or an "it's okay" from her, but the opposite happened. She actually wriggled away as she lowered her legs and yelled, "Get out, get out!" I ejaculated on her stomach the moment I came out of her, filling up her navel. Lying back, satisfied, she smiled into the void like a fool. Despite it all.

I left after breakfast, after reading the *Chicago Tribune*. I gave her a fake address and phone number when I kissed her goodbye.

Before leaving Chicago, a city that did not want me, and going up to Grand Rapids to finish my K, I wanted to enrich my cultural life. I had two choices before me: the Art Institute of Chicago with its Velásquez paintings, or *Robin Hood, Prince of Thieves* with Kevin Costner, which was playing across the city.

The museum was closer. I wasn't prepared and they should have warned us of the danger. I had always wanted to see the famous painting *Las Meninas* for myself, but it had been loaned to a European museum and in its place was a small cardboard reproduction testifying to its location. It wasn't until I was leaving that room that I saw human greatness for the first time in my life: *The Pietà* by Tiziano Vecellio. Titian. An almost square painting, his last, the one that he wanted to offer in exchange for his own burial at Venice's highly coveted church, the Santa Maria Gloriosa dei Frari. On loan from the Galeria dell'Accademia, the painting is a world heritage masterpiece that leaves Italy only twice every one hundred years. The entombment of Christ after the descent from the cross. From near or from far, any Westerner will recognize Christ lying dead in the arms of a woman: the Virgin. But it is the other woman, the distraught Mary Magdalene, who draws our attention.

I don't know her yet, but she will come. My own Mary Magdalene. She will resemble Titian's Mary and I will believe in her.

For the first time in life, I felt my legs turn to jelly. I had to remind myself to breathe before I was overcome by an unknown force. A yearning to believe, like a summer thirst. A temptation. Could that be me, that nearly naked, inanimate body surrounded by a world both real and symbolic?

I have not desecrated anything yet. I am not that man with the pierced hands and feet. I am not Christ. For a long time, I believed that I was. But today I know, from all those miracles I do not perform, that I am not. The disappointment made way for love. I believe.

I backed away from the painting until I reached the room's exit, kilometres away, and went to a bench in the middle of the next room without which I would have fallen to the floor in terror of something totally unfamiliar. My year zero. I believed she would be dark with pale eyes. Lively. Beautiful and strong like the night. I would have to wait a little longer. But she would come, that much I knew.

It was October 30, 1991. From that day on, I wanted to have Faith. Inhabited by that Maeterlinck phrase that I liked so much but the significance of which I never understood until now: "The greatness of man is measured by the mysteries he cultivates, or before which he stops short." Pious hopes. My mystery will be to learn what or whom I will love.

Two years later.

I am standing under the shower, drinking the hot water and pissing at the same time. I've always peed in the shower. It's the only place where I don't have to aim or hold onto my dick. Sometimes a hot, acrid and spicy odour rises up through the water and steam.

I just quit the Grand Séminaire de Montréal where I've been studying since returning from Chicago and I'm washing it off me. I will never be pope. I know I would have been a good and good-looking pope. I was only seven when John Paul I died and John Paul II was born to the papacy. How handsome and imposing, that man all in white! Spic and span and looking like a rock star. Men of faith – real ones – have an extraordinary sense of style. So unique you'd think they were aliens. I will not be among them. There are just some things that you know and can do nothing to change. And besides, I have American Indian blood and centuries will always separate the colonized from the conquerors.

The American band Bad Religion just launched their album called *Recipe for Hate*. Dissident music that condemns – and justifies a burgeoning hatred for America. From within its borders. Someone also tried to take down the World Trade Center's twin towers by setting off a bomb in one of the underground levels. I would have handled it differently. And I would have succeeded.

At first I was reduced to resignation but then I understood more clearly. I no longer have that corporate faith that makes us climb higher. Or rather, there's a limit to true faith and it's fragile in my case. Life is so ingenious sometimes. I advance sideways, like a crab.

In the second John Paul's case, I believed that he had it. And that I didn't. That was probably my first act of self-sabotage. I hadn't yet learned that our own destruction exists within us. Checkpoints, even the most concrete, will not work for me. Besides which, at twenty-three, I believed I would always be able to get married and live the way people do in brochures on happiness, even though my religious allegiances and aspirations would not allow it. Or rather, they did. I could always choose to continue ejaculating on and into women on the sly, even if my morals would not get used to that. I considered excommunicating myself, but a Protestant pope? That's not happening any time soon. Anyway, I'd already peed into a baptismal font, and since I was going to have to confess to it, I preferred keeping this outrage to myself. At the end of the day, we are designed so that we always manage to find our way in any situation. In happiness or in misery for some, and in a back-and-forth movement between the two for others. Between indifference and devotion. Ever since excuses became reasons, humanity has advanced like a man who is drunk and blames the error of his ways on drunkenness.

ON THE FLY
A young man in his mid-twenties, with reddish hair, walks down the sidewalk running alongside the Marie-Reine-du-Monde Cathedral and goes in the back entrance of a building that should

be the sacristy but which is actually the archdiocese of Montreal.
He looks at his watch, walks down the vast grey terrazzo corridor,
through the second floor's odours of damp dust and burnt wax,
and passes by a series of identical tall doors with transoms. He
knocks on one of them, probably hears a response, and enters.

"Monseigneur Vecellio."

Monseigneur Vecellio got up. A white man of Italian origin with almost Nordic colouring. He was allergic to the sun and an ecclesiastic career was better suited for this condition than that of, say, a lifeguard.

"Mr. Morris, come in, come in. Your punctuality is a virtue, young man. It's a sign of humility that, sadly, many lack."

He turned around after we shook hands. It had been two years since we had agreed upon it: no gesture of respect to his title or to the Prince of the Church's ring he wore. He looked outside, still standing, and said in a rather cheerful voice because he knew the reason for my visit, "So?"

But I did not answer right away.

Upon my return to Grand Rapids, after finishing the K in early November 1991 and despite the fact that the session had already started, I registered in the seminary. Goodbye to cooking. The whole enchilada. I believed as firmly and sincerely as possible that I was going to become a priest, a father, an abbot. Assigned to two or three rural parishes, I would write and make myself known to my bosses, the higher clergy.

Theology, study of the Scriptures, learning Latin. Elements, Syntax, Method, Versification, Great Literature, Rhetoric, Philosophy I, Philosophy II...

They had assigned me an old Capuchin father, who was very nice but out of touch and who fortunately died just before Christmas. Life is ingenious, I said to myself again upon learning of his passing. I had started to read Calvin more seriously and was obsessed with the polarization of my existence between Good and Evil. I was convinced that this concept could explain the understanding of human nature that I was constructing through my very small self and the episodes of grace and disrespect that were guiding me on a journey that had previously been only abstract.

Entering the seminary confirmed that my thinking could find refuge only in the pendulum's extremities. The middle was of no interest: it was never at rest. I remembered my grandmother's old clock and its little plastic cuckoo bird with impossibly coloured feathers that came out to announce the hours, and I clearly saw the futility of the middle: the swinging weight has nothing to do with the centre. The distance between right and left marks out time and stimulates its passage. I went to bed when the cuckoo clock chimed seven times, and through the open door, I saw this birdhouse with its big and little hands and the numbers whose workings I did not understand. I knew that the longer I waited, the more cuckoos there were. Eight, nine, sometimes ten. I thought it would crow like that forever, up to an infinite number of cuckoos, like when I asked my mother how high you could count. The next morning, without making a fuss or even reconsidering it, I heard the bird call out the same number of times as he had the night before. I was five years old, and a five-year-old's grasp of time is one that I will never decipher.

To one day be Pope. In this ascent that I so desired, I even saw myself serving as a missionary to the Third World for a few years, winning points for charity and learning a couple of exotic languages. Earning Pope Miles. We already knew then how intense Catholic fervour was in Latin America. Calvin and the very simple duality of the human spirit. Up to this day, still and forever as foolishly maintained by both cowboy and Indian, Superman and the bad guys from the planet Krypton, the Galactic Alliance and the forces of evil in *Star Wars*. I was wrong, like the majority of contemporary philosophers. We will never be able to define ourselves so simplistically. Unless we see an upside to it. Like America.

So Calvin was dispatched. Been there, done that. They had quickly put me on the path of Bishop Vecellio, who had been working hard on Saint Augustine's Manichaean period.

I really like coincidences. They've almost always given me good reason to. To this day, I have a post card of Tiziano Vecellio's *Pietà* taped to my fridge. I met two Vecellios in one year. Coincidences are impossible to refute and that always reminds me how important poetry's uselessness is. We can agree: rhymes serve absolutely no purpose at all and yet we love them.

The several-centuries-old work by the painter Vecellio and the meeting with a bishop bearing the same name made the most absolute of rhymes. What's more, I had instantly taken a liking to this man because he was secretly writing a work on the cult of masculinity in the Vatican's religious artworks. In these paintings, the men are always naked and the women always absent, save for the Virgin Mary, who is always clothed. "Phenomenal manipulation and propaganda for the power of men," he'd said. He'd made me read his imposing thesis of over seven hundred illustrated pages, on which he had been working since he became the apostolate's assistant secretary late in 1969. From Etruscan art to the great Crusades, from the colonial conquests to this Empire's specific domains, the planet's richest and most magnificent collection of art is found at the Vatican. And the entire collection has one guideline: its opening quotation, the phrase borrowed from Goebbels, German Propaganda Minister for the Third Reich: "If you tell a lie big enough and keep repeating it, people will eventually come to believe it."

I will not tell myself often enough to have Faith. I still believe that it will come just as my love for Emma came to me. And if that's what it takes, even if I'm a hundred years old, whether it strikes like lightning or creeps in like mildew, I will respect it and offer it my gratitude.

As I do Emma.

On the road back from Grand Rapids, passing through Chicago. I had taken a break near O'Hare Airport. That's where I got what I thought to be a second sign. Thanksgiving 1991, millions of Americans migrating as families – inhabitants of a country I was beginning to despise.

A string of aircraft waiting on the tarmac and a fascinating queue of jets in the sky, lining up above the runway. As I watched these little floating crosses approaching runway 270, I believed that I had faith and that my life would therefore be simple at last. Monothematic. Devoted. Finally. Devoted to a single idea, a single concept, a single purpose: the quest for forgiveness, even if I was unaware of the sin. It seemed easy to have but one goal: for my financial situation to be resolved immediately, for this nascent consumption of women to have been only a brief moment of distraction and folly. I would have tried to stop doubting. One goal: to be assigned my human duty, my mission, with no surprises. For Friday afternoons to always be happier than Monday mornings. Fuck the job and fuck the boss. I'd be normal.

I would have enjoyed being a prisoner, voluntarily during the week and paroled on weekends. In medicine, I would have become a specialist in a clinic, most likely a urologist. Never any emergencies, for consultation by appointment only. Clean little interventions, almost no blood, in the calm and muted atmosphere of a private clinic. From Monday to Friday noon. Dinner with friends on Saturday, to justify the alcohol. Hungover on Sunday like hospital recovery rooms after a surgery.

For a long time, I also thought that the life of a garbageman would be simple and perfect. You get dressed at dawn, you hang onto the back of a truck for eight hours, tossing in tons of trash, and at the end of the day you go home, get undressed, eat supper and watch TV until you go to sleep only to get up the next day to do it all again. A dream. But, always that eternal echo of reason, I surely would have counted all the bags and cursed our overconsumption. The idea lasted until the evening when a childhood friend – a garbageman by trade – stated, upon coming home and sitting in front of the television with a beer in his hand, that his boxers were crawling with little white maggots. White worms are okay, but when they become flies, they are no longer acceptable because they just breed more little white maggots. That's when the survival of a breed that I consider to be useless begins to drive me crazy.

My epiphany before the painting at the Art Institute of Chicago had awakened my admiration for the beautiful. I saw beauty everywhere: in urban sprawl, in cement, in anonymous eyes and even in a dried-up sandwich. The Stendhal syndrome. Confusion and a questioning of everything. And all those planes in a gigantic, logical, controlled improvisation, each in turn provoking a state of grace that I had interpreted as a call to eternal faith. I think it was Woody Allen who said, "Eternity is very long."

That call would last two years.

"So?"

He waited.

"What's this terribly serious thing you have to tell me today?"

Then he sat, indicating with his right hand for me to sit in his well-worn Italian chair. Dating from the turn of the century and covered in shabby leather, it had come from the Biri Grande house, a lone relic of a noble but bygone era. Waiting. In silence. An immense mirror hanging behind him reflected my image back at me, proud and courageous in this defeat.

We could have separated right then and there. We both knew that he had understood. I believed at that moment that it was strangely like breaking up with a lover. The situation did not require more words but an involuntary mechanism kept us talking anyway. Now, looking back, I know that it was a loving relationship – that a man can love another man.

I have the utmost respect for people who figure things out without having to endure the flood of useless words. Those awkward words that stick like muddy footprints on a clean floor, that turn into those surreal sentences between two lovers no longer in love or even those futile phrases of condolence in response to someone's sorrow. I knew that the administrative procedure for my withdrawal-discontinuation did not interest him. A second, two, three and then a full minute passed without either of us moving a muscle. One long minute that lasted ninety seconds.

You can make an erection disappear by squeezing your legs together.

I was the one who broke the silence.

"I want to have faith, Pietro." We spoke to each other in formal French but I called him by his first name. "But it doesn't come. I'd like to be like you and accept this phenomenon like a necessity and a miracle. I'd like to have no more questions, to kill all my spirit's doubts and move straight ahead on a single path."

I shook my head and softly exhaled through my nose.

"I'm fed up with not having it. I thought this commitment would solidify the little bit of true faith I already had."

One second, two seconds, three seconds.

"But I can't have it only part-time."

He didn't answer, perhaps verifying whether or not the echo of what I had just said would repeat the same thing until there was silence again. The street and its muffled noises could be heard in the background.

Understood. Capiche. Time to move on. It felt like someone had pulled the trigger of a gun.

"I have a favour to ask, Marc."

"Yes, Pietro."

Without having guessed at the effort that this service would require or the shape of the memory it would one day take. A memory that survives to this day.

"I have a German friend from my time as a student in Munich and he'd like to go hunting. Naturally, I assumed you'd enjoy showing him a few birds. It's an old promise."

"But the season for hunting migratory birds is over."

"I know. Does that pose a problem?"

"Of course not."

I didn't smile but it seemed to me that I restrained myself. "We'll meet at 4:30 tomorrow morning in front of your place, Pietro." And thus my commitment to the Church was discharged.

The next day. Bang. Dull thud against the backdrop of a cobalt sky.

The sun was about to rise, black turning blue just before daybreak. Little crosses flitted in every direction, landing in front of us by the hundreds. Teals. The whistling and the gentle landings on the water announced their presence well before we could see them. Shooting down a bird in flight is one of the nicest shots you can take. I watched the empty casing floating, still hot and smoking, at the edge of the pond.

I whispered, "Monsignor Maastzinger."

I could just as easily have shouted because the Cardinal's shot, which came without warning, had stunned me as if I'd been hit by a high-speed train. I had only my strident

"Ey-iiiiiiiiiiiiiiii", screamed at the top of my lungs, for ambient noise. And the intoxicating and comforting odour of burnt gunpowder.

"Monsignor, we don't shoot blue-winged summer teals, we're not allowed to hunt them this year."

But I told him as a mere formality, a nervous gesture, because I'd been so surprised by my hunting companion's visual acuity. In any case, all hunting was illegal at that time of year. It was still dark.

"I know." Bang bang, he answered, shouldering his gun and firing two more shots that were followed by the muted plop of something falling into the water.

The two little flightless ducks floated upside down about four metres from our shelter. A dead bird on the surface of the water bears a strange resemblance to a bath towel lying on the floor. Bang, bang. Another blue-winged summer teal.

Thus ended my orders. With a Cardinal who came to vacation in Montreal and absolutely wanted to go hunting. He looked like the Evil Emperor from *Star Wars*, the same eyes and that willful look of a man who never hears the word 'no.' I was not about to disappoint either one. Exactly three minutes and forty-four seconds later – I had set my stopwatch – nineteen empty cartridges floated next to us, thirteen blue-winged summer teal and just one with green wings.

"That's enough, young man, you're a marvelous shot. I got only half of them," he said in very clear French as he laid a hand on my left forearm, near the watch on which I had seen the seconds tick by. We collected the birds and the empty cartridges and returned to Montreal with a hunting bag fit for a king.

The next evening, I was invited in my role as former apprentice chef, and now as former man of the Church, to prepare the birds for Pietro and Maastzinger. Peking teal. Like the famous Chinese duck but adapted to our land. Hosting with and taking inspiration from champagne, a bottle of Krug Grande Cuvée. Six little blue-winged teals, hunted illegally. They aren't gutted; it's criminal to remove the taste of a game bird's innards. Blanched once to properly separate the skin from the flesh and to pluck them more easily. Hung at room temperature so that the skin dries completely. That's the secret to Peking duck. Only then do you remove the insides, which are perforated by little lead pellets and have already started to smell and to flavour the flesh. You don't rinse the birds after the guts are removed. I stuffed them with an onion, a stalk of celery, a carrot and a good cup of maple sugar and baked them uncovered in the oven for an hour and a half, basting the skin every ten minutes with maple syrup into which I had crushed wild juniper berries. The result was a spectacular shiny amber varnish that formed a thin caramelized crust on the birds' crispy skin.

From the ducks' skin, I made bite-size morsels that peeled like an orange. You have to baste a small rice crêpe with hoisin sauce and add thin slices of cucumber and finely chopped shallots. One or two pieces of duck skin and you roll it all up.

We did not discuss my "defection" again; instead we talked about the recipe for head cheese made by the mother of Cardinal Maastzinger, for whom – aside from the pig's teeth and skull – everything was fair game. "We do the same thing," I replied, "but with moose."

More than two years after he began his pontificate, I remembered the odd conversation we'd had that night about the existence of God as it is defined by the Christian Church.

Maastzinger: "Men created an image of God based on their own comprehension of humanity. Like in a business, an admirable model of belief and devotion, the operational structure of our God is made up of a chief executive, vice presidents, directors, employees, a marketed product and the people who buy it. It is both the limit and the logic of the human spirit to entrust itself to the mystical. That's just the way it is. And after Pius IX in 1870, the papacy became infallible. Don't you even have a boulevard named for him here in Montreal?"

He bit into his rolled crêpe and continued with his mouth full.

"And it's fine that way. Much easier than trying to understand why, for example, this present moment is precious because this meal is delicious. If we spent all our time trying to understand and envision the present, we'd always be late for the future and unable to imagine ourselves somewhere else.

To have faith, young man, you have to look far ahead and avoid doubts."

He paused and then went on. "You should always demand the best of everything. Meals, wines, friendships, faith included. The conformity of an average is the worst human atrocity I have ever had to witness. Satan, if he exists," he said, raising his eyes to the ceiling, "is no longer requiring anything but a comfortable minimum of yourself. Find out what you are and own it."

That was his only comment on my decision. Certainly, like a snake on a road, I understood that there is no answer to Faith and that perhaps the very source of its power is in its inability to offer any alternative solution when it fails. In any case, it was and still is an admirable demonstration of a human spirit to want to explain that which cannot be.

Me: "If everything is so perfectly perfect, wouldn't we automatically have this faith? A snake that wants to cross the road should flee from danger when a car passes in front of it. If the snake relies on its retreat to keep it safe, it has a better chance of passing safely between two cars than if it waits for the coast to be clear and then arrives right smack in the middle of the road just when the next car comes by, right?"

Pietro: "So there has to be one who guides the others who are in danger of losing their lives."

Maastzinger: "One who understands the rhythm of the road and can come to the aid of the others, and so on."

Me: "So they aren't all qualified to cross the road?"

Maastzinger: "Certainly not. There is no equality among souls, and Faith is the justice for this. Justice was invented by man on the basis of an egalitarian principle. Faith is egalitarian because of its Reason."

I was paralyzed and could not answer at all. This conversation was being held at a level far superior to mine. I like to play with the big boys. I did it in elementary and in high school. Sometimes successfully, other times less so. But that's where I also learned that silence proved me right, nine times out of ten.

Maastzinger again: "But your problem is something else completely, young man. One day, you will understand that Reason is not in conflict with Faith, but rather that it completes it."

He emptied his glass.

"Saint Thomas Aquinas wasn't just a misogynist. He also wrote great things about the reconciliation of Reason and Faith. Be patient and open, your consciousness will exist entirely in the present."

This idea bewildered me. I didn't have the energy to embark upon a complex thought process and I chose to remain silent as I refilled our wineglasses. I was like a man who knows he is drunk: I didn't open my mouth because I was feeling loose-lipped and knew it would betray me.

Perched on a teak pedestal table behind Vecellio was a photograph of him sitting at a table and talking with John Paul II. Like a trophy, I thought to myself, and I hate trophies.

I continued to listen rather than to hear, staring at the snapshot. Maastzinger knew that his words carried weight.

He took another sip of the Saint-Vivant 1990, which was one of the 24,026 bottles produced by Domaine Romanée Conti that year. He offered a final thought. "Saint Augustine was almost right, except on the question of original sin. I suspect that sin of being one only for men."

Pietro seemed to silently agree. I would not begin to understand until years later. To my great relief, we had gone on with the meal, discussing the news, olive oil and the best smoked meat in Montreal.

To follow the glazed duck, I cut up and sautéed the meat with broccoli and shallots. I used an authentic Chinese wok over a charcoal fire, which perfumed the mixture and blended pleasantly with the scent of spices I wasn't familiar with. I was frying the food, my hands still smelling of the fresh wild duck, and in the rising steam I pictured Émilie, the night before at her place, her knees on the floor and her belly flat against the sofa. She had kept her blouse on, I think because she was embarrassed by her small breasts. Caviar.

We made love. The TV left on for background noise. On the evening news, a rerun of a report on an RCMP raid on the Mohawks at Kanesatake. Contraband cigarettes. Where I lived.

But I didn't hear the rest because she got up from between my legs and knelt down facing the sofa. Seeing her from behind, her butt arching toward me. Just a few minutes after having penetrated her, I'd had to close my eyes because I wouldn't be able to last much longer. I couldn't see her eyes, only the brown locks of her damp hair and her arms above her head. And that scent of sex: mint, pepper, coriander, a mixture of sea salt, algae and salty herbs. Millennia of bestiality are still within me. My mind looks at a woman's ass or breasts and physical reactions are set in motion. At CEGEP, I read Françoise Dolto, Gloria Steinem and Simone de Beauvoir. It's a lost cause. Purposeful knowledge and the idea of intelligence have nothing to do with cell memory or what we will soon discover: biological instinct.

I was erect and far too excited. I had to think about something else: how many kilometres were on the pickup's odometer? How do you sharpen a good knife? I didn't know that Lebanon was such a small country. Israel and Gaza, Eve's sons. Did the people who made the Sears catalogue know to what extent the ladies' undergarments section shaped several generations of young boys and men? Apparently, toothpaste is in fact a fraud that actually promotes tooth decay. Wood from the cedar tree is rot-proof. I always thought that before the 1960s, life was in black and white.

And I pulled out of her to breathe for a minute. She made sounds that I interpreted as being imploring. Wanting to be back inside her, I put more force into it and I listened. She didn't say no, but she groaned with her mouth closed. She used her hand and began calmly pushing and pulling my thigh to her own rhythm. When I saw myself in her in that instant, with the beads of sweat, as beautiful as the fragrance of meat, in the hollow of her spine, I felt like an all-powerful mammal. In a controlled frenzy of aggression, I would have staved her in from sheer happiness and a few seconds before ejaculating, I really wanted to ask her to marry me. Two minutes later, I no longer wanted to. Sorry, Émilie, it's not you, it's me. I want to marry someone else. Especially now that the hard-on is gone. I went back home, claiming the urgency of having to prepare my things for my hunt with Maastzinger the next morning.

I made a consommé from the duck's carcass, boiling the bones with onion, celery and salt. I served it very clear in a bowl at the end of the meal.

I had chosen to study Calvin, to expand on his thinking, but instead it was on his predecessor Saint Augustine that I had built all my doubts and those two years in the seminary. "If I am mistaken, it is because I exist."

This idea that says a man cannot save himself, the one that also says that man, if left on his own, cannot free himself from the temptations of concupiscence. Is desire to be condemned? And at what point does Freud enter into this story?

Pietro Vecellio, for all his grandeur, had one flaw: he was incredibly paranoid and saw conspiracies everywhere. But today I believe, as I did for all those unverifiable suspicions, that he was almost always right. "There isn't any more humanity today than there was at the dawn of prehistoric times."

There are just many more people now.

ON THE FLY
Dozens of people wait in line on a sidewalk in front of a business establishment. Couples and singles. Young and old, mixed together. Some are talking and others wait in silence. A man of the Church stands alone as he waits in the line in front of Schwartz's, the Jewish delicatessen on Montreal's Saint Lawrence Boulevard. He collapses, victim of an illness. Passersby quickly surround him and offer their help. He is unsteady but he gets up on his own.

It was 1993 and Cardinal Maastzinger was going to leave Munich to become Cardinal Bishop of Velletri-Segni, before being named guardian of the Congregation of the Doctrine of the Faith at the Vatican. He recovered from a little stroke, but his vision was permanently affected. He never went hunting again.

Three years later. I'm still searching. I find little because I'm looking too hard.

I got back on the FUCK YOU route. I was at the top left of the Y, near Sault Ste. Marie, in this little Ontario town where the residents had burned Quebec flags the year before, during the referendum of 1995.

To be more specific, I was on a little island called Saint Joseph Island, in a canal north of Lake Huron called North Canal. The Hurons had always been the enemies of the Iroquois and the Mohawks. I no longer felt much of this bellicose coexistence that had haunted my ancestors' daily life for centuries. Might this even lead us to believe that there's a chance for peace in the Middle East? Since time began, America's founding peoples have also been warring neighbours. In the twentieth century, they understood that by joining forces they could get more out of the white man's colonization. But the colonizers took everything. My land, sucked dry by the empire. My own land. You entice me and yet I am ashamed to set foot on your soil. I would prefer to fly far above you.

At the end of October, it turns cold and the rain no longer falls down from the sky, but falls sideways, almost horizontally, because of the strength of the gusting wind. Very close to the geographical centre of the continent, in the American Midwest, between two mountain ranges, the prairies give the wind thousands of miles to gather momentum. Here the clouds never leave the sky except well off into the west.

Over the past three years, I made so much money selling contraband cigarettes that I finally got sick of it. No more object of desire.

The companies were complicit. We were told when the delivery trucks would leave the factory and the guys from Akwesasne easily robbed them after waving down the drivers. In return, bribes were paid to a few factory execs in the U.S. We bought the cargo for peanuts from Big Dan, the guy responsible for "jumping" the trucks. He weighed in at 345 pounds. The transactions took place just across from Cornwall or in Saint-Régis, on Lake Saint-François, opposite Akwesasne. Under cover of night, we'd load the cartons of cigarettes onto a speedboat headed to the towns of Sainte-Barbe and Saint-Anicet, Quebec, so we could resell them for a high price to middlemen, or to Whites right there on the reservation.

I owned four cars in less than three years, including a Ferrari Modena 360 with a glass engine cover. A stiff, dried-up roadster that bounced my ass all over the road. I resold it for cash to the same guy who ended up getting stuck with my tobacco business. The car is philosophically impossible to drive because the envy of others grows into a familiarity that I am beginning to abhor. At every shopping centre, strangers descend and want to talk to you, urging you to rev the engine and burn rubber. All the young guys in baseball caps want to race: it's been inscribed in the history of humanity from Ben Hur to the Formula 1, including the first tricycle that we straddle at the age of two. For a few months, I dated a girl who painted her nails Ferrari red. Her toenails, too. I was afraid. So I left her.

I became a misanthrope, resenting the admiration of others. Once I had taken the measure of this human hierarchy, I wanted to set myself apart from it. I did not want to belong to this powerful, materialistic caste. Seeing how false a woman's reasons for wanting to be loved could be, I wanted to find true love with one. The Ferrari, in my case, was well worth the *Summa Theologica* by Saint Thomas Aquinas, the same saint who bequeathed to History a work entitled *On the Inferiority of Women*.

Six gears, 420 horsepower and 300 kilometres per hour later, I was 26 and I found another 1987 Dakota pickup in a scrapyard on Laurentian Boulevard in Laval. Eighteen hundred dollars. That made me happy. I sold whatever could be seen: houses, boats, cars and other gas-burning machines. I invested everything in a company that manufactured semiconductors in Ottawa, laundering my cash in exchange houses, which were then controlled by foreign banks not subject to the mandatory declarations of cash. There is nothing illegal about acts that aren't yet against the law.

At the corner of Peel and Sainte Catherine, my paper money was transformed into a bit of electronic data that passed through the Cayman Islands before returning in due form to Montreal, where it filled a Canadian public securities account. Averaging a commission of 3.74 per cent, I "transferred" the sum of 40,000 dollars over 41 consecutive days. All perfectly legal. The practice was discovered a few months later and a draft law would soon require the declaration of any movement of cash totalling 10,000 dollars or more. I was always one step ahead of the laws I had chosen to obey.

I was the last passenger on a merry-go-round. The last client served.

By the dawn of the new century, I looked like I was going to be disgustingly rich, on paper at least. That was before everything collapsed in the spring of 2000. But, content in this misfortune, I would already have given it all away anonymously because I would be in love with Emma.

Emma, who did not like tablecloths. She held them in fierce contempt. "I have the right to be demanding, it's as simple as that," she said whenever I saw her remove the cloths and reset the tables at the restaurants where we ate, *sans* tablecloth. I smiled. I would forgive her anything.

The Catholic principle of guilt strongly motivated me. I immediately liked the idea of confession. It's like taking a shower. The cleanliness of the soul, which is soothed through this act, allowed me to start over from scratch thousands of times. And square one is full of hope and goodwill. Like when you say, "I do." I wanted to love like when you're famished. I also had the urge to cook for people. My projects became efforts to procure happiness. To prolong it. To get extra time. I had put my FUCK YOU on ice for three years. Today, I went back to it.

ON THE FLY

Saint Joseph Island. Lake Huron. The waves are almost two metres high. A motorboat. One man in front and another in back. They are bending overboard and hauling in a net by hand. From time to time, they stop and one of them stands and harpoons enormous bony fish that look prehistoric. Some are kept while others are thrown back into the water. Some return to the bottom and others float on their side.

The end of October now. Lake Huron. The rain nipped at my skin like tiny pebbles thrown in my face. If I stopped to wiggle my fingers, they'd freeze. I was bent over the edge of the motorboat, prevented from falling into the water by the mountaineering harness I wore. The sturgeons that we brought in from the nets strung two days earlier weighed between ten and ninety kilos. The smallest, the ones we called netters because they usually slipped through the mesh of commercial nets, were systematically thrown back: they didn't have eggs. Every once in a while I kept one to send to my mother, to remind her of the sturgeon stew she used to make for me when I was a boy. Netters from the Saint Lawrence River were generally caught by sports fishermen. It was very rare that you brought one in without breaking all your tackle, especially since they always put up a memorable fight, quite the party every time. I would make one for Yolanta later that night.

You keep only the female sturgeons. Sometimes the motorboat was loaded and heavy, with several dozen fish tightly wedged together. Because of the bad weather that day, we were heading in early to remove the eggs.

Sheltered from the wind and waves, we harvested the eggs on a wooden trestle set up in a boathouse. Each female sturgeon, easily identified by her egg-laying orifice, was laid out and held on two scaffolds above a milk pail. We reproduced the way gravel and pebbles rub against her underbelly and the eggs thus expelled were collected. We harvested over three gallons, fifteen litres.

We rinsed the sticky liquid, filtered it and removed the fatty tissue and membrane before covering it with a thin layer of non-iodized salt so that the eggs wouldn't turn yellow. We kept only the translucent little grey-green beads. The deeper the lake and the greater its exchange of water, the better the caviar. Small and mid-sized bodies of water give the roe a muddy taste so its value plummets. That's why we fished for these eggs in the Great Lakes, in a protected wildlife reserve: North Canal's shores and spawning grounds lie on gravel beds.

When I was younger, I fished hundreds of pounds of roe under the Mercier Bridge, west of Montreal, across from the Kahnawake reservation. No one knows about it. As good as Russian, maybe even better. As it does for wine, the label of origin increases the value of all things already familiar to us. It's a basic principle, an added-value. Our expectation regarding a thing makes it truer, even if it's based on a lie.

We then packed the roe in white metal containers that looked like little cans of shoe polish. We sent them through the port of Montreal with a label reading "Sevruga, Produce of Iran, Caspian Sea." From there, the little eggs travelled back across the Great Lakes and ended up on the tables of hotels and big restaurants in the north-east: Chicago, New York, Boston, Washington, Philadelphia. Dear America. In love with Iran because of its caviar and its oil. Too bad it's inhabited. If America ever found it had that much oil, I would provide the caviar for the nouveau riche.

Yolanta is my second cousin, daughter of the cousin who fished for sturgeon with me. I think her father knew that we knew each other in a more or less biblical sense. He didn't say anything because between what we want and what we imagine, imagination always wins out. And he did not want to imagine.

I think I could have loved that girl. I seriously asked myself that question because I truly wanted to belong, once and for all, to that select group of people who meet each other, get married, have children and live happily ever after. The last time I'd seen Yolanta, she'd been only sixteen. Although my desires were not dictated by the legalization of an act, I found her to be much more liberated and desirable at twenty-two. When she was sixteen with breasts rising up to her throat, the idea of knowing she was straitlaced and nervous did not appeal to me. But now she had a certain grace and her movements were much more fluid and sensual. I never slept with her. We exchanged a few caresses, nothing more. I would have liked to see my desire for her increase, but it didn't.

There are cows of the same breed, born of the same bull and mother, that give fifteen litres of milk a day and others that give forty. Breeds that give fatty milk and others that give lean. You mustn't force things. Take what comes, as it comes. Fortunately, this is a mechanism that still operates outside of science. Less and less, however, since these days cows are selected according to the size of their udders.

We went back to my cousin's with our little containers of caviar, which would leave for Montreal the next morning, and a netter that I planned to cook the way my mother did.

I sliced the little sturgeon into thick steaks, leaving the skin on because the fat – source of all the flavour – was attached to it. I put the fish into a huge Dutch oven with five big round onions, a dozen round potatoes, six chicken legs with their skin, a litre of 35% cream and a pound of butter and seasoned it with salt and pepper. I covered it all with water and let it simmer for at least two and a half hours. The result, as baroque as it was medieval, was spectacular. Precisely midway through the cooking process, the fish and chicken skins came off the meat and rose to the top.

Apparently Yolanta, who had helped us pot the caviar, did not have the same digestive facility with the stew as the two men who had hauled in nets full of fish in the storm, in four degree Celsius weather. The only fattier, more indigestible thing I have ever eaten was a mille-feuille of eel and foie gras that I myself had created while completing a three-week apprenticeship at Robuchon's restaurant in France the summer following my one and only year at the Institut d'hôtellerie.

For the entrée, I made blini with buckwheat flour. We spread the pancakes with a lightly whipped fennel-flavoured cream before spreading a good centimetre-thick layer of fresh caviar over another one of softened butter. I still don't understand why caviar is good.

Yolanta slapped me. Faster than lightning, she rose from her chair and lunged. I froze and she gave me the most surprising smack of my life. I would have forced a kiss on her. I would have taken her head and neck between my hands and brought her mouth to mine. Not for long, just a quick kiss. Maybe she would have opened her lips. Maybe she would have been willing and sweet. I'll never know because tears were pouring from my left eye. I had just told her that, aside from a polite two or three minutes at most, I wasn't interested in having any conversation whatsoever with a woman whose bones I didn't want to jump. Exit, out. My blini and its caviar came out through my nose. "Bastard, stupid male pig. How can you be so juvenile?" Yolanta shouted, along with a hail of insults that I couldn't understand. Her father, my mother's cousin, was doubled over and laughing hysterically. He caught his breath and called out his wife's name: "Semyhé!" Then he was off again, "AAAAAHAHAHAHAH! Semy! AAAAHAHA."

The fact remains that, back then, I was already beginning to wonder if this state of desire would last my entire life. What happens after a man is castrated? The same thing that happens to a chicken or a pig? He stops thinking about sex and puts on weight? I remembered that my mother used to castrate the little suckling pigs we used to breed on the reservation. She held the little pig upside down between her legs. With three fingers of her left hand, she pulled gently on the two little testicles, and with a barber's razor in her right, she cut them off with one swift, careful flourish. The piglet squealed for a good minute or two and then he went on with his life as if nothing had happened. Castrated.

I clearly saw that I was incapable of sublimating my desire for any and all women who were intelligent or pretty, or a combination of the two. Especially then. I thought or felt that her particular beauty wouldn't last too long. I needed more.

My desire had to be sustained by something more conscious and intellectual. I didn't give a damn if she was married, separated, a widow or a mother, happy or not. A fundamental desire to conquer. I had to believe that I could leave my present life for this other one. Each time. And it took much less than two minutes to figure that out. It was not only about the need to ejaculate, which is, in any case, rather easy and trouble-free. It was a question of knowing that I had been desired and feeling that I had been chosen. Perhaps Yolanta was held back by those invisible filters that protect us from so much worry and bother. From the honesty that earned me a hand across the face, she learned where my sentiments lay. I like situations to be clear, particularly my own.

I would be thirty-eight the first time I told a woman she was beautiful without desiring her.

Are all the events in our lives connected? How does human justice work? Does it exist? If, for example, I steal an old man's walker, will I automatically be punished by some moral authority? I am making an abstraction of civil or criminal justice, one that involves more of a social contract. I'm thinking instead of each individual's personal and flexible sense of justice.

Who makes the rules? Is it a matter of education? Karma? Religion? Belief? How do we change our own rules without causing too much damage? I did not respond to Yolanta's slap because I believed it to be just punishment for my comment. I got slapped for having said it, not for having thought it. And

I was not one for self-flagellation even if I had always admired the idea of doing penance. It may seem twisted because its physical brutality is so visually spectacular, but self-flagellation is a rather lucid effort to bring what we truly are into line with what we believe to be right.

There are ideas that I have on the one hand and those that I express on the other. Encounters between them rarely end well.

When we subtract the true Self, what we would *like* to be, from all that is inconsequential, we find our human identity. Our Identity. The closer the value to zero, the closer we are to finding happiness. I am not a poacher because I seek vengeance or want to do something bad, but because my nature requires me to break the rules that others have made. I would later learn that we don't change as we get older: we only become more and more of what we truly are.

I always did like the smell of skunk piss.

End of November. Didn't have sex with Yolanta.
End of the sturgeon spawn. I left again heading south.
Rudyard to St-Ignace to Mackinaw City to Vanderbilt to
Gaylord to Grayling to Roscommon on Route 75. I avoided
Detroit, the most criminal city in the white man's America,
choosing instead to take a detour of a few kilometres and
thirty minutes through Ann Arbor, the most bourgeois university city in white America. I told myself that since I was
hating, I would go to the ugliest place I could think of: a rich,
sanctimonious suburb.

The Americans had just elected a very young president, a
lawyer, Governor of Arkansas Bill Clinton. This little town
lives sheltered from real life, protected by the halo of UM, the
University of Michigan. Famous for a faculty of law attended
only by the rich white elite and sometimes by a few minority
students, black or light yellow, who have to prove they deserve
to get in.

I was about fifty kilometres from Detroit, far enough
away to be out of range of the dissident words of the young
rapper Marshall Mathers, otherwise known as Eminem. And
now the poster for Nirvana's *From the Muddy Banks of the
Wishkah* was hanging in a music shop window. It was the
group's second album since Cobain had died the most beautiful of all America's deaths, as a victim of an alleged conspir-
acy. As if the empire could not have been founded on anything other than the assassination of its powerful men, men
who never died like the common man. Martin Luther King,

the Kennedy brothers... And they were predicting the same fate for this young, Southern president who did more than just look smart. Why don't powerful people ever die the way blue collar workers do?

Of course we would later find out about that intern's famous blowjob, which made Clinton look bad for a few weeks, not because he'd been unfaithful, but because he'd gotten caught. Not so smart after all. But in the end, the story reassures us about human nature, telling us that even the king of the world is just like us. And so the flaw rose to the surface.

I wanted to sleep in Ann Arbor. I met a girl in a greasy spoon. I sat at the counter, leaving an empty seat between us. Like the law of urinals in a public restroom: if several are free, you never stand right next to a guy who is already peeing. You follow the odd numbers rule. He pisses in number one; you skip number two and use number three.

Forcing love, particularly with women, is called rape. And it's the women who decide. Consent comes from breasts. Mammals.

I ordered two eggs. The waitress disappeared for a few minutes and then returned with my eggs cooked sunny-side up. I cannot eat slimy eggs. I love cracking an egg and sliding the uncooked yolk and white between my fingers, but I am unable to consume a translucent egg white. My innate embarrassment would have forced me to swallow them. I don't like making mistakes and I don't like pointing them out; it's so discouraging. I would have eaten them, blocking my nose from the inside, blinking my eyes and swallowing without chewing at all.

The waitress must have noticed my expression. I was obviously ill at ease.

"You should have said so."

She took away my plate. I smiled and said, "Thanks you."

Because of my grammar mistake – the 's' had no business being there, I knew, but I was nervous speaking English that morning – Emma turned toward me and murmured, "Over easy."

I would have liked to answer her. Zero. Memory erased. Turn off the machine and start again. Reboot.

"*Saterihwaienstha ken?*" Are you a student?

That was all I could think of to say, something in my mother tongue.

She didn't seem surprised. And she nodded yes without being too sure of what I had asked. I think she liked not understanding. I repeated my question in English, telling her that it might be easy to ask for her hand in marriage. It was her turn to remain silent for a moment. Then she answered that in her lifetime, she had said no much more often than yes. I also asked her if she had read Flaubert.

"Don't worry, if one day I end up loving you the way I think I might," I thought, "I'll have you read all the great classics. I'll even have you read aloud on Sunday mornings."

We talked while I ate my eggs over easy, not sunny-side up. In fact, I listened to her describe her term project on the bioethics of cloning. She was studying law at the University of Michigan. Four months earlier, an entirely cloned and viable lamb named Dolly had been born in England. We exchanged our contact information. She seemed to be somewhat interested. I was completely blown away.

I wondered what she might find interesting about a French-Canadian, half-Mohawk guy with no real ambition and a battered pickup truck. I wanted to believe in her so I stopped being suspicious. A man and a woman between the ages of eighteen and forty do not casually trade phone numbers. That's the procreative age group. With all the ambiguity surrounding the survival of the race and social dictates. But forgetting becomes voluntary and genuine. It's stronger than we are.

Emma Souquet. French father from Haute-Savoie. He had been working at the Tour de France when he met Natalie Jones-Ricci, the doctor for an American team. He followed her to Chicago and they had three children. Emma is the eldest.

Average size, brown hair, thin but not bony, muscular from running. Hazel eyes. I remember getting lost in those eyes. I told myself, "She's the one." And yet we held back. It was like an alarm system. A protective measure.

Before I left the greasy spoon, our eyes met in the dirty mirror hanging behind the waitress. Looks that said we understood. I knew that she knew. But I thought I'd also seen that look on Julia Roberts in *Pretty Woman*. Or was it in Titian's *Pietà*? I'm having more and more difficulty recognizing significant things: I perceive everything as being important and that misleads me. When should we truly believe in the thing we want so badly? I wanted to have faith. I want to love a woman. It will come. I know that I know it. Even if I'd learned to be suspicious. Especially of myself. So I fell in love with girls on every sidewalk in the land. My psalms. Later I would learn that faith is like love: they are both states that exist without our knowledge and I find that reassuring. I'm glad that the Greek Era is mythological and part of the past. I would have loved too many gods. It's easier today: one Christian god, one Muslim god and one Buddhist god. One single woman. For me, the singular simplifies hope, making it accessible.

If only Emma would be my faith! I was ready. But I was also the exact opposite of her life. I would have to pay attention. I left Ann Arbor that morning anyway. I am slow to understand the things that are important and essential – the things I want.

But I could hardly tell her that I loved her after only fifteen minutes. Even if it were true. So many truths make us seem crazy. My courage will come later.

I headed south to Columbus and then, like a migrating bird, I drove back north the way I'd come, to a Detroit suburb where I got a flat tire. An hour-long break forced me to retrace my steps and take a detour through Ann Arbor. A flat just at the split in the Y was more than a coincidence. If I went east, I'd hit Detroit and my path would continue; if I went west, I would be choosing Ann Arbor and that girl Emma from the University of Michigan. A traffic light and a green sign. Make a choice.

I decided to go west, betting my marbles on the girl. Retracing my steps was a violation of my ethos, so I changed religions. A man in the service of what he believes to be love sacrifices some of his honour.

I didn't find Emma again. Four thousand, two hundred and forty-seven kilometres from North Canal. Seven whole days spent randomly searching the streets for her, thereby confirming my sudden obsession with this woman. Like Titian's painting. Another calling. A stronger one.

No answer when I called the telephone number she had scrawled with a make-up pencil between the 'w' and the 'o' of the word 'welcome' printed on a grey, butter-stained napkin. No luck, no accidentally falling in love. Providence and destiny were not there, not this time. And yet I believed in them like you believe in your horoscope when you want it to make sense.

December, 1996. End of the Y. Toronto.

We can never guess the origins of the events that enlighten our lives. I sold my pickup with the intention of giving up this itinerary. I was disappointed that I had not seen Emma again. FUCK Y is certainly better than nothing. It could be an abbreviation for any number of words. Yolanta, for example. Tristan's Yseult – Isolde, to those who read such tales in English.

Or the Y chromosome itself. I hate genetics because it has usurped our mystical understanding of the world. It's obvious that something more precise will be found in the future, that as technology progresses, our knowledge of the reign of carbon will narrow in on a centre that is increasingly minute. And we are such gigantic little things.

I sold – finally practically gave away – my second Dakota to a Chinese-American, a used-car salesman at the corner of Spadina and Queen Street. Three hundred and fifty dollars. The price of a good red Burgundy and a one-way ticket to Montreal.

ON THE FLY

A man walks south along Spadina Avenue. He slows his pace and looks at two women who are examining Chinese fruits at a sidewalk stand five metres away. He stops for a second. Nothing unusual. He hesitates. You can see his pulse beating in his temples. He turns his back in the opposite direction and begins walking again, with some difficulty. He does another about-face and approaches the two women,

who are handing money to the vendor in exchange for a bag of litchis.
He stands behind one of them and his lips are moving.

"Will you marry me?"

She turned toward me. She looked at her friend. At least six times, silently. Then she asked, "What's your name again?"

But she remembered my name perfectly well because she had left me a dozen messages on my old cassette answering machine between the time we'd first met and that day.

Together, Emma and I are going to experience all the days that punctuate human lives. Case closed. I secretly hoped, for the first time, that she would be stronger than my faith. I truly love her. With all the hope I can muster. And hope has made more people live and die than all the wars and illnesses known to man. It seems that love is a normal, even necessary characteristic of the human condition. I had reached this exit off the highway.

She didn't answer my question, but she did smile. Her friend quietly left her side, disappeared, and we walked for a good half hour before saying anything at all. A woman's silence can be as precious and dangerous as a prayer.

We spent our first evening together talking late into the night. About nothing and everything. Particularly about everything, but also about my recipe for maple syrup madeleines. She didn't know about madeleines or Proust.

This time is not lost, Emma. At sunrise, I asked, "*Teshahwishenhe: ion hen?*" Are you tired?

She had immediately wanted to reply, signalling with her hand for me to wait. And with a slight hesitation, she said "*Hen Tewakhwihshenheion.*" Yes, I'm tired.

At that moment, I really knew. I couldn't doubt it anymore.

I didn't leave for Montreal that morning but several days later, while Emma went back to her family in Chicago for the Christmas and New Year's holidays. In January 1997, she registered for the next session of her master's program at McGill and moved in with me in Montreal. She quickly spoke an impeccable international French, which she already knew to a certain extent because of her father, and even a few more words of Mohawk.

We both said, "*Kathontats.*" I consent.

For a long time, I believed that money could help me dodge the difficulties of life and make it sweeter. Even with all that cash, I wanted to belong to the world, a clear sign that I wasn't a genuine rich man. I worked for a year as an assistant cook in a Mafia restaurant on Saint Lawrence Boulevard. I was in love.

October 12, 1999. Montreal.

Elmyna turned two last week. I hadn't gone hunting in two and a half years. I had replaced gunshots with words of love. That morning, I drove her to daycare. She hadn't had any accidents the night before so Emma put a sticker on each hand, a butterfly on the right and a silver soccer ball on the left.

Between the car and the coatroom cubby where I hung her white knit coat, she lost the ball sticker. When she went to show her rewards to her teacher, she noticed that she was missing one. She instantly looked disappointed and she turned back to me.

"Wait, Myna, go with your friends and I'll go look for your sticker in the car."

I found the little soccer ball in the parking lot, thereby becoming a toddler's hero. She regarded me with such admiration that I felt proud and momentarily forgot what was in the trunk of the car.

October 12, 9:45 a.m. He had arranged to meet me in the Costco parking lot, near the Victoria Bridge. The sun would meet no obstacles that morning. Not a cloud in the sky and the moon was still visible. A radio newscaster announced that in Sarajevo, the six-billionth human had been born. At the dawn of the millennium, clever United Nations officials in New York – who were completely out of touch with reality and overdosing on the symbolic optimism only bureaucrats can have – decided to slap a number on a child born in what would be "Gabriel" city, host to a religious and ideological polarization that would last at least another century. Serbs. Croats. Bosnians. Faith, once again.

I don't waste time thinking about this nonsense anymore because I'm a happy daddy. Happiness is like Fentanyl in an operating room: for just a few minutes, it freezes faith and the fear of living.

When Emma and I moved in together, we bought an old industrial building in Park Extension where they used to make cosmetics for women. Carelessly warehoused and certainly forgotten in its basement were aluminum barrels with pictograms clearly indicating a danger: skulls and warnings about noxious fumes. Three barrels of acetone. One hundred and thirty-five gallons, more than four hundred litres of a product normally used for nail polish removal or some other liquefying function. I made at least fifteen calls to the poison control centre, Public Security and private companies that reclaimed dangerous materials, but no one could tell me how to dispose of it. Until that October morning when I sold the stuff for next to nothing to a friend of a friend of a friend who knew that I had it. Acetone can be used for a variety of things: it's most often used to dilute plastics, epoxy glue and floor varnishes.

I knew that this isomer stabilizes nitroglycerine and makes it more resistant to shock during transport. My chemistry classes, which were also helpful in the kitchen, served me once more, and it's a good thing they did! The guy who wanted to buy the stuff from me also knew it. A rendezvous in an anonymous parking lot, two dark-eyed men, and I understood. The guys looked North-African. They were the ones who had picked the Costco. I liked the symbolism. They loaded the metal drums into their Jeep Cherokee's hatchback, gave me five hundred dollars all in twenties and waited for me to stow the straps in my car and close the trunk. Just before getting back into my car, I yelled, "For a trip with no turbulence, make it four to one."

The following December 14th, the guy was arrested in the state of Washington. The trunk of his car held seventy-seven kilos of more or less stabilized nitroglycerine that had been rendered rather harmless by four times too much acetone. At the very beginning of the investigation, telling the truth seemed preferable, until they realized how much better the catastrophe scenario would serve the cause. So the reassuring man from the CIA never again spoke openly about the miscalculation of the chemical mixture. Thanks to the Freedom of Information Act that came into force years later, the facts would be made public.

I had sold him at least three times more than what was found. I no longer ask myself where the rest might be. Nowadays, I just don't care.

I like to think that this schmuck reversed the proportions of four parts of nitrate to one of acetone and mixed one part nitrate with four of acetone. Despite all the media hype, the security alert and the invention of American paranoia, Ahmed Ressam's explosive mixture would only have irritated a few eyes. I definitely would have been named an accomplice and associated with acts of terrorism. With a failed act, no less. So that is my second worst nightmare. The first being that, during a stay in central Africa, I fall victim to an unknown disease that will, for all eternity, bear my name.

This act made me happy. After two full years of being "among the ranks of humans," I had the impression that my life was repeating itself and losing intensity. My doubts as to the use of that acetone made me feel more alive.

My life now resembled what I had wished it to be when I decided to believe in Emma. But like a stretched-out rubber band, my original shape had a great deal of memory. There was an original state that was hard to forget. That's the memory. Memories: they're pretty much everything else and they try to make you forget your original state.

Twenty-five twenty-dollar bills. Sometimes love is a Bible in the bedside table drawer in a seedy motel.

I love Emma because she always wipes the bottom of her nose with her hand twenty times when she finishes an espresso. I love this woman because when we go cycling, she stops from time to time along the road and bends over the side-view mirror of a random car to look at herself and check the condition of her face. Whether the car is parked or just waiting at a traffic light. If I am driving along one day and a woman does that, I'll plant a kiss on her mouth. I do believe that for two years and without meaning to, she almost cured me of my irrational need to complete the route I had undertaken. For a long time, I asked myself if this was a good thing or a bad one.

When I think of her in silence, she is a thousand times better replacement for prayer.

Are the days when I don't buy a lottery ticket the ones when I would have won?

I hit the road again.

Emma did not want to plumb the motives for my itinerary. By dint of her of love, I assume. When I left that night, after having stopped to get our daughter at daycare, Emma was wearing her hair up so that it looked like a palm tree on top of her head. I thought it looked fabulous. I told her she was beautiful. For all the times she might have asked. It gives the greatest pleasure when it's volunteered. She didn't try to figure out why I was going to hunt again after a two-year hiatus. Because I wanted to finish writing the FUCK YOU from my atlas?

Plenty of questions are left unanswered, implying an understanding of the universe. Most of the time, this will be misleading. I seek and I try not to create too much meaning. Seeking provides the same benefits as running for the sake of running: endorphins and the easing of a guilty conscience. I am, on this continent, a native. I believe I am owed the right to genuine rebellion.

"I don't know, I hope I'll find the answer on this trip." But she still had not asked the question. Doing things with no goal in mind is a luxury that most people cannot afford.

I kissed Myna's neck, my nose cold against her warm skin. She hooked her hand around the nape of my neck and pulled me to her.

"I love you, sweetie."

"Kiss, Papa," and she licked my cheek.

Montreal – Mont-Laurier – Maniwaki. Five hundred kilometres of reflection. I didn't fall in love with Emma. And I
don't think she fell in love with me. We decided to be in love.
Like lightning. It never strikes by chance. Science tells us that
the phenomenon is created by a polarized charge that is invisible to the human eye. A negative pole attracts a positive
charge. Love must also evolve.

A minimum of affinities is enough for two entities
entirely unknown to each other to decide to become one.
Love is not a state that exists entirely independent of our lives.
Nor is destiny. There are states that should not be understood
because the evidence is overwhelming.

"Maniwaki 19 km." A dead porcupine lay at the base of the
sign, one more bit of roadkill. Smashing Pumpkins in the CD
player.

Do any of us know how much happiness passes by us,
barely touching us because we prefer to avoid the reefs?
Emma did not exist to be my lover, no more than I did for her.
It's not about the essential nature of a being, an innate characteristic or a matter of DNA. Her presence in that little
restaurant in Ann Arbor was just her life. Her daily routine,
independent of mine.

My life, motived by my own body's unique hunger, led me
to stop at that very place, not because I would find a woman
to love there, but perhaps because just as I was passing in
front of it, the man who stops there every morning for

breakfast had to rush off to work because he'd just realized his watch had stopped. He left a parking place free directly across from Al's Breakfast All Day. Maybe he would stop to buy a new battery at a drugstore along the way. These incidents were not connected. Such unknown trajectories reveal nothing at all. How can we continue believing in some sort of pre-destination if we don't see it as an integral part of the human's primitive structures? Are Jansenism and its opposite synchronized by their opposition?

What if nothing is connected? I tame death by hunting. I scoff at my own end. But it is so early.

I arrived in Wakefield, a few minutes from Maniwaki, before all of that year's deer hunters. Far from the anonymity of big cities, poaching is a trivial, everyday and, most importantly, a silent affair. You learn a lot more from a poacher than from a retired hunter because silence always confirms the uncertainty.

I rented a boxy little chalet made out of plywood and minimally furnished: a wood-burning stove, a gas range and fridge, a sink supplying water that gutters installed just under the roof had collected in a forty-five-gallon barrel. One early morning out of two, the water stored in the black plastic barrel was frozen. I had to either anticipate the problem or wait until the noonday sun melted the ice.

The nights announced the snow to come. There was a hollowness to the air and the winds from the north were getting stronger. Halloween was only a few days away. The deer hunting season would open on Saturday morning, half an hour before sunrise. For several hours, it would seem like there was a war going on. The sound of hundreds of shots being fired would be heard from tens of miles around.

The night before, on Friday, I took down a buck.

Saturday morning. The season officially opened. The sun was just appearing on the horizon. The light for the hunt was still a pale violet. The day was about to begin. I was sitting on a cold spindly chair. I heard the wood crackling in the old Norland cast-iron stove and the gunshots outside mingled with the noise of burning logs.

The cabin smelled of dead mice and humidity. The old floor was cold and dirty. There was a tarp with curling corners and I was sure it had not always been grey. A steamy fog rose up from my cup of coffee and dissipated a few dozen centimetres away. Through the window, I saw the tree where hunters usually hang deer they've slaughtered. A gallows. I wanted to know what it meant to be dead. To be in the deer's place, no more than meat. To be reduced, once and for all, to an arrangement of cells. It would be simpler for everyone.

I left my buck hidden in the forest overnight. It had taken all my strength to haul it up at the end of a cable, high enough so that no coyote, wolf or bear could come and eat it.

For whatever it's worth, I peed on the tree, under the animal. It seems that the scent of human urine keeps wild animals at bay. If our urine contains molecules of what we eat, then coyotes, wolves and bears must not be big fans of clown shit because the only food I'd eaten the night before I went hunting was from McDonald's. I don't know what they put in it but I love stuffing my face with that food. It tastes good! They say, and I'm apt to believe, that McDo's "amalgam" – a bizarre mélange of industrial meat, oil, enriched flour, salt, sugar, "secret" sauce and other sandwich ingredients – is absolutely and scientifically impossible for the human stomach to digest. At least not when combined in this form. It is so bad that they also mix in drugs to prevent vomiting. Pietro found this information on the Internet.

That won't keep me from eating it again. I'm quite happy to know that they are looking after my health by preventing me from puking every time I eat their stuff. I had long believed that "fast food" meant that it was prepared quickly. You order and snap, it's ready. In my case, it's more about quantifying the speed at which I ingurgitate the merchandise. Like a dog, keeping chewing to a strict minimum. Or like a child who eats an oyster in front of the grown-ups who are watching and waiting. The oyster should be a Catholic sacrament at adolescence.

I toasted bread on the stove. Buttered slices spread with jams that Emma had made from groundcherries and lemon zest. My communion. As good as a shower after a day spent shovelling manure.

I pulled on a hunting shirt and went out to make a call from the inn. My little cabin didn't even have running water. Certainly no electricity. No cell phone service and no toilet.

As I covered the hundred metres between my cabin and the inn, I passed the proprietor's garden, where an abundance of fine herbs were still growing. I felt the urge to cook and I went to leave a message for the stockbroker who managed my investments, asking him to sell everything and convert the money to cash because I would have some things to take care of in the week ahead. I repeated the order to sell three times.

Had I not seen that garden, I would not have opened a restaurant. For a few seconds, I had the desire to cook for other people and that was all it took. Cooking is closer to pure generosity than making love.

And that was how exactly 11,827,341 dollars and 3 cents were anonymously donated to three charitable organizations: one for unwed mothers, one for the homeless and one for breakfasts. I love you, Emma. The letter explaining this gesture insisted that nothing be said on the subject. And aside from one news item published in a big Montreal daily on November 11, 1999, nothing was disclosed. I had kept a little over a hundred thousand dollars because, in my desire to become a mature, responsible adult like the ones you see in TV ads, I hoped to have a legal and legitimizing business to keep me busy.

There naturally comes a time when you feel that you should be responsible. When you are awakened each night by the scary feeling of not knowing why you exist, it is time to numb yourself with strong doses of future, hope and projects. I had to try. So many people and so many stories say that normal life means having a family, plans for the future, a social identity, legitimate hopes for happiness, a dog or a cat, a reason to get up in the morning. It is also imperative to be passionate about something: bridge, electric trains, scrapbooking, your car, knitting, cooking or even, in the worst-case scenario, the movies.

I understood that the more things I had to do, the less I would stray. The sight of winter thyme, tarragon, rosemary, chervil and sage had called me to action.

I entered the inn and Mrs. Parker came to see who had opened the door so early and especially to find out who had been the first to take down a deer that morning.

"Did you kill one?" she asked me.

"Yeah, this morning, just as you leave here, on the 118. There was a gorgeous buck, an eight-pointer, in the middle of the road. I came down and he didn't move – I had just enough time to shoulder my gun and fire."

She listened with the most reverent attention, as if she had been waiting for this moment all year. I took up the story again when I saw that she wanted to hear more.

"He died about a hundred feet into the woods. I came in to eat and call my wife to tell her. I'll go back after and get him."

I hoped she hadn't heard my conversation with the broker's answering machine. And then she said in all sincerity, "Congratulations! I'm gonna go see it just before my hunters come back in at noon."

I don't know if she believed me and I never will. Silent understandings such as these were probably common around there and I was the one who was being a bit paranoid. My buck had not died on the road.

I have always known that 12 times 12 equals 144. On the other hand, I don't know what eleven times twelve equals. I also don't know why I can't retain this information. The life of deer is fairly predictable. That much I do know, and it often costs them their lives.

The night before, I had pretended to bait an area with apples. Nothing more normal than a hunter baiting his territory during hunting season. Orange vest and feedbag on my back. The sack should have held about fifty pounds of apples, but in their place was a Proline bow and three hunting arrows adorned with razor-sharp blades. I located a trail often taken by Virginia deer, the real name for white-tailed deer. Their autumn paths are never the same as their winter or summer ones. Animals are familiar with their environment and know full well that their survival depends heavily on year-round access to food. I swept away the dry, crackling leaves at the foot of an immense beech and sat down. The beech grows in climax forests, where they remain at a perpetual zenith until some outside force comes along to disrupt the ecosystem. It replaces the maples, birch trees and oaks because its dense foliage prevents the sunlight from reaching other species' struggling saplings while its own grow more rapidly than all the others', making it hostile to the trees that once grew there. Besides, its bark makes me think of a woman's leg under her skirt in autumn.

I must have fallen asleep for ten minutes or so: when I opened my eyes, the light's intensity had changed. Ninety per cent of big game hunting is done in the half-hour after sunrise and the half-hour before sunset. A total of one hour when animals die. I was immobile. I adopted the rhythm of the forest, I melted into it and became part of it, as invisible as its billions of trees.

Nothing moved of its own accord. Only the wind imprinting a slow, coordinated movement on the forest. Nothing but an animal. It's the most spectacular arrhythmia there is, impossible to miss. The sudden appearance of animal life before you is the closest you can get to the Stendhal syndrome: an emotion so unexpected and surreal that the brain needs a few seconds to adapt itself to this new reality. A revelation for believers. For normal folk, an illumination whose virtues we extol.

Forest. Trees. Earth and sky.

It was a lone female. Followed by another one with her fawn. Both were constantly looking behind them, stopping and pivoting their necks, the ears alert and anxious. I knew.

The females are less fearful. They lead the way. They are the infantry, the foot soldiers, cannon fodder for the big males. The bucks follow in the does' footsteps. They survive thanks to this instinct of fear and suspicion, believing that the danger is always in front of them. Somewhere between a female and themselves. Always. Still.

I didn't move. The two females and the fawn stayed a few dozen metres from me for five or six minutes. In the calm order that would be completely disrupted once the courting period, the rut, began. No more solidarity. No more between males than between females. These same females would violently chase away their babies during the few days of the mating season.

The survival of the species is dictated by clashes and confrontations that are indisputable and often violent. Even when two males fight over a rutting female that they've been following for days, there is no guarantee that the winner will mate. The victor will have the right to offer himself first, but it is still always the female who chooses. And she just might choose the loser. In this case, if another female in heat chooses the same male at the same time, the two females will also fight a violent battle. The defeated doe leaves and the male will mount the winner. And thus proceeds an order of things established thousands of years ago by heaven knows who or by what.

Could it be love, Emma? A simple enough sentiment for the human race. Emma is particularly shrewd when it comes to discovering that another woman is interested in me, even if it's in the most ordinary way. That, too, is written into their system.

According to popular belief, it is mainly the big dominant males who reproduce, thus assuring the strength and majesty of the race. Reality tells quite a different story. A longitudinal study conducted over more than ten years by a Michigan veterinary school investigated the reproductive behaviour of Virginia deer. It showed that the big dominant bucks are so busy using all their strength to preserve and defend their territory that they are exhausted when they come to the rut and are unable to "service" more than two or three females. Meanwhile, the males with less imposing antlers will successfully cover anywhere from six to twelve females. And the quicker ones reproduce the most. Premature ejaculation is good for the entire race and favours its survival.

To be more precise, these adult male deer have a gland in their mouth that is more highly developed than the one in the big trophy males. The so-called Jacobson's organ enables them to detect a female's ovulation and arrive at just the right time. And to leave more rapidly to seek out another female once the first is inseminated. The mammal kingdom, to which I belong, is more confusing than I was led to believe.

What if men saw their women only long enough to ensure the species' survival? Working hard all winter. Mating in the spring. Ten thousand years of evolution of the species to realize that, even if the quantity increases – there will soon be seven billion of us – the quality of humans remains the same. Do we have this Jacobson's organ, too?

Didn't they once keep the boys away from the girls until they became young adults?

ON THE FLY

A man wearing camouflage gear and a balaclava is sitting with his back against a tree's smooth grey bark. The leaves are not on the branches anymore but are lying dried up on the ground. The man is almost invisible. Almost motionless. He moves very slowly and stares straight ahead. He holds a bow and raises it to aim at a male deer that approaches, nose to the ground. The man's breathing accelerates. He draws his bow and holds it that way for quite some time.

As expected, the male followed.

Khena'khwaye'wenta's. Calm down.

He had waited until the two females and the fawn were far ahead before making his appearance. He sniffed the earth, worried, nervous and unable to remain still. As he turned and lowered his head for a few seconds, I grabbed my bow and drew an arrow. A monstrous dose of adrenalin pumped through me. The performance of a fundamental act is still registered in our genes. Hunting for food. Quite a few centuries ago, this stopped being necessary for our survival, which is now otherwise assured by agriculture and industrialization. How do we rid ourselves of the innate need to reproduce? Pietro would have said that it's through religion.

Is this intoxication perhaps due to our capacity to kill? Hunting is also the love of death. How do I release myself from this genetic memory? We do not premeditate the death of a fly the same way we do the death of a large mammal.

I shot the arrow when the deer was twenty-one metres from where I sat.

I always enjoyed measuring the distances between myself and other things. Three feet four inches, twenty-four and a half feet, one metre eighty. Eleven beers. Forty ounces of vodka. It's even better when there's eighths or sixteenths of an inch. At school, they taught me the metric system although in everyday life, the American system prevailed. My penis is seven inches, not seventeen point five centimetres long. All men have measured their penises at some point in their life.

One hundred miles an hour is faster than one hundred and sixty kilometres an hour, even if it's the same speed. Fifteen miles to the gallon, not six litres per hundred kilometres. I also prefer to cook with cups and teaspoons rather than with the quarter litre and its millilitres. Those little measurements are just too French.

I calculate metres only with the bow and arrow. They made us take archery classes for the permit accreditation, placing the test targets ten, twenty, twenty-five and thirty metres away. When I shoot arrows, I kill the animal in metres;

when I fire a gun, I aim at sixty, eighty or two hundred feet. I have a split personality.

I held the drawn arrow for a good thirty seconds before releasing it. You start to tremble from lack of strength if you hold your aim for more than thirty seconds. After a quick assessment of the distance, which I thought to be about twenty metres, I took my third sighting at a point behind the animal's left front leg and raised my bow a bit to aim for the lungs. I exhaled slowly to keep from shaking and I let the arrow fly. You have to let go at the very end of the exhalation, just before taking another breath. That is the calmest moment and the most accurate. Important things are also said after releasing a big breath. "I don't love you anymore, I have cancer, I'm going to die..." The army's elite snipers know that they have the best chance of killing the targeted man if they wait for the end of their breath.

It's like a little drumbeat followed by a whistling and an almost immediate *tchack*. You don't see the arrow. I kept my eyes open to observe the animal's behaviour. If he is startled and runs tail down, he will die. If he flees tail up, it means he wasn't wounded, at least not mortally. Mine jumped, turned around, and fled, tail down, in the direction from which he had come. A seriously injured animal always goes back to where it came from. It retreats on its most recent footsteps.

My temples were pounding, the way they had when I'd seen Emma again on that street in Toronto. Even when I know that the noise is internal, I have a hard time believing that no one else can hear it. It's hot and cold all at once, you can start to twitch nervously and you breathe through your mouth. My lungs projected a steaming mist fifteen feet in front of me. Using the measurement for arrows, that's five metres.

It was imperative that I stay calm. Note the last place I had seen the animal. And wait. An interminable thirty minutes not knowing if the animal was dead. That's the time you allow for the deer to bleed out and die. Where? How? Far?

No matter where I am, I can't wait long. Since I thought I had aimed well, I went looking after only twenty minutes. I want to see death. It cheers me up. And excites me. I crane my neck when I pass an accident on the road. A big part of my thanatological education, aside from the funeral parlour, the flowers and the church, had come from a series of films entitled *Faces of Death*, in which they present "live" deaths and the disposal of human remains post mortem. Hypnotic. Always the feet. Television shows them whenever someone dies in a public place. The body is covered with a yellow cloth but the feet are often sticking out from under it.

I found my arrow planted in the earth quite far away, intact but bright red from the point to the notch. Still slimy. Sticky. Bright red means oxygenated blood. I had hit the lungs. I was happy but not yet entirely so. Crimson droplets coloured the dead leaves under my feet.

Thoughts flew into my mind of their own volition as I tracked my prey. "I'm a scent hound after blood. The drops line up, forming a path that leads somewhere. They're getting bigger and bigger. Now the earth is churned up and stained. The blood looks like caramel. Young shrubs are also marked with red. Here the blood is foamy, exactly like bubble bath or a raspberry juice emulsion. Air mixed with blood into an emulsion of death. I test its smell: the tang of iron again."

The buck had pawed the earth and found the humus. The end of a life is not elegant. He must have wheeled around, panicked and dizzy. I thought of my Uncle Jean-Paul on his deathbed on Isle-aux-Grues, moaning, eyes rolled back, convulsing and calling his father's name before that final exhalation. I prefer the blow to be swift and direct, followed by a fall I'm unaware of.

The animal tried to clog up the holes left by the arrow with leaves and earth. Soil can plug wounds and staunch the flow of blood. He pads himself with humus, leaves and twigs and recovers. Not this time.

I raised my eyes. He was directly in front of me. Brown with a white belly, dead. Stretched out with his head hidden under a fallen tree, as if hiding this final effort to survive. I saw his hooves. I was weightless: an astronaut. A state of grace that lasted only a few seconds. Killing is as powerful as an orgasm.

I pulled the dead deer up onto a small rise. First I had to hold the penis and testicles firmly and cut them off – there is nothing like this in the entire universe and my mother had taught me how – taking care not to detach them from the body. I left it all attached to the urinary tract, which leads all the way to the bladder and must not be allowed to drip urine on the animal.

Next I cut the anus, this muscle-sphincter, from the outside, inserting two fingers to spread it and get a proper sense of its shape. The blade must gently follow its contour. Another story about guts. And you have to do it without cutting yourself.

Some Chinese eat pig anus. I imagine it tastes something like spiced calamari. I adore deer testicles, poached and then fried in hazelnut butter and Espelette chili peppers.

You cannot imitate the sound of a knife slitting skin that wants to be split. The only sound anything like it is made when a slightly dull blade shaves off a man's stubble or when a woman shaves her legs in the stillness of her bath.

The abdomen begins to swell immediately after the animal's death. Millions and billions of bacteria work in symbiosis while an organism is alive. As soon as the symbiotic relationship ends – and here it depends on a very precisely regulated temperature – the bacteria cease functioning and life ferments. My knife released the straining skin with nothing more than the pressure of the weight of the blade.

I pulled at the steaming paunch and organs. The slope helped with the runoff of blood and the removal of the internal organs. Another slice of the knife detached the heart, which was attached to the thorax in a web, as well as to the lungs and liver. Another cut for the diaphragm, or the top skirt as it is called when served on a dinner plate. One last cut to sever the windpipe from inside. Everything came out; the animal was empty. It was steaming. Now it was a carcass, smelling of blood. My hands were full of it and I was proud of my red hands. I was never afraid. Even of love. It's nothing when we love. It's like one more proof. My cock is not what makes the difference.

My arms were red up to the elbows. I wiped the sweat off my forehead with a stained, rolled-up sleeve. I planted my knife in the ground, like a dagger, to clean it. I attached the deer by his antlers and hoisted him up on a branch, as high as I could. The rear hooves dangled above the ground. I had no strength left. Water ran off me into the earth; steam rose off me into the sky. I was a mist.

I tried to pee on the tree. There was still some liquid in me. Then I went back to the cabin to sleep.

Hunting season would open the next morning.

It's up to only a few males in almost the entire mammal kingdom to ensure the survival of the species. The males have nothing to do with raising their young. Nothing to do with conjugal fidelity and nothing to do with the females of their species, save for three weeks out of the year. This system does not cause them any distress, no more than does their species' risk of extinction. That's just the way it works.

I remembered one of my conversations with Pietro. I understand your conclusions, old friend. Your vow of abstinence had not been a stranger to this fact.

There is nothing more intelligent than a human being who does not procreate because he knows he will weaken his lineage. The contrary also happens to be the stupidest idea in the world. And a jerk who has kids because he thinks he's smart? We don't even think about it anymore, it leads to war. We have children because that's how it's done, regardless of our value or our merits.

As planned, Mrs. Parker came to see my buck. She offered her heartfelt congratulations and I was touched.

"Could I cook you something for supper?" I asked.

"Uh, sure," she answered. She was definitely surprised and not quite convinced that a man could "make food" as well as she could.

I cooked the whole haunch of the deer. I encased it in pastry dough and served it with herbs, meat glaze and garlic confit. There must have been enough for fifteen people. The meat had not aged. It's always better to let it age. Muscle fibre takes longer to die than the soul or the mind. That's necrosis: the enzymes become active, flavouring and tenderizing the meat. As a result, the meat is improved by the taste of the fat. The fibre itself has almost no taste at all, so the flavour comes only from the fat content. It takes a few hours to age chicken or guinea pigs and days to age the "big ones." Fat is the key to the flavour.

We quickly forget that it takes time for meat to become good to eat. Venison is an exception because it is already highly flavoured by its diet of wild, natural foods. I remember eating a porterhouse steak at Peter Luger in Brooklyn, the world's oldest steakhouse. They dry-age their cow and beef steaks for forty-one days, otherwise they'd be tasteless. The entire menu can be summed up as follows: steak for one, steak for two, steak for three, steak for four. No credit cards. Cash only. Impossible to go without reserving weeks in advance.

Steak is a natural symbol of success that dates back to pre-historic times. Centuries ago, Emma, when we were still wearing animal pelts, I brought meat home for you. And now I invite you to a restaurant where I buy it instead. Beef still tastes good. We'll serve real meat in the restaurant that is opening soon.

I'm sure that even human muscles, if properly aged, could be delicious. We wouldn't know the difference. Except for old-man meat. That, I imagine, would taste of kidney.

I cooked. I was happy and I didn't think about my family. Three hunters who returned with a doe that they hadn't yet skinned and butchered came in saying that something smelled good.

"There's enough here for your supper, if you want."

As he left the kitchen, the last one said, "Well, we're going to take care of this lovely female first, Mrs. Parker."

They had killed a doe so I called out, "Did she have a calf with her?"

"Not sure, just a minute...Jacques, did she have a calf on her tail, the female?"

I didn't understand Jacques' answer but he nodded yes. I dropped everything as I ran, taking Mrs. Parker's best knife with me and following the three men out to their pickup.

"Can I ask you something?"

They didn't answer. I guess that a guy with a pink Banana Republic tee shirt and a butcher knife in his hand does little to inspire conversation. They said yes.

I cut off the doe's udder, taking every precaution. It was intact and full of milk that was still almost hot, only slightly cooled.

I drank three beers while I prepared the udder. Anxiety makes me drink. Like during the hockey team's elimination series. When Emma tells me we have to talk. Or when I'm frustrated. Alcohol sometimes helps wash life down your throat.

After briefly cooking the udder in the oven to curdle the milk, you carefully remove the skin. You're left with a pink, veined, translucent pocket through which you can see the hardened white liquid. I sautéed it in raw milk butter over a hot flame, no more than fifteen seconds on each side, and then I made tiny slits on the top and inserted pine needles and a drop of vanilla.

It was as fragile as a lightly poached egg. I put it back in the oven for thirty minutes, but since I was so impatient, it may actually have been only twenty. A pinch of salt. Served like a slice of pie, it was more tender and silky than foie gras and so exquisite that I didn't want to make one ever again. The memory of it will come back to me whenever I kiss a woman's breast.

Mrs. Parker and the three hunters told me it was good but that the haunch was better. They had seconds and thirds of the meat and added at least ten times more salt. Haunch and mashed potatoes. They thought I was weird until they learned that I was half-Indian. Even without aging, the meat was perfect. With the help of a little instruction in anatomy as I explained the muscle fibres and the parts of this deer "thigh" to them, I had eaten the knuckle in a single bite. The wine was disgusting.

I wished them all a good evening, and that same night I left the inn with my pickup and a deer that was missing a buttock and a hind leg. I was thinking about making a dry-cured ham with the other buttock, the way they do it with pigs in Spain. Jamón Serrano. And about opening a restaurant.

ON THE FLY

Saturday night, in an isolated northern village, a pickup with a dead deer loaded into the back comes to a stop at a traffic light before getting onto the highway. Green, yellow, red. Green, yellow, red. The stop is longer than usual. Its turn signal indicates a right turn toward the on-ramp but the vehicle finally continues, going through the intersection and parking in front of a bar where a woman's silhouette fashioned from pink neon sputters.

It smelled of stale cigarette smoke. The odour had even permeated the ceramic tiles on the floor. A suspended ceiling. Music louder than a conversation. Seated men looked at a small lit stage where a girl in a bathing suit and high heels was dancing to the rhythm of the music. I also sat down and watched. Once the embarrassment passed, I counted at least a dozen of these girls and only a few more clients, all men. The girls were seated at the bar. I felt I was being examined and evaluated. A waitress, wearing clothes, asked me what I would like to have.

"A Bud and a green crème de menthe," I said as over the speakers came the voice of Ozzy Osbourne singing to his mother that he was coming back home.

I had never ordered that before. I hate crème de menthe. I don't know why my nerves make me do such strange things. I say things when I'm nervous that I would never say otherwise. When I manage to say them at all.

She turned around and quickly came back with my order on a plastic tray. She put it on the table with a clean ashtray.

"Twelve-fifty," she told me after doing her calculations in a voice just loud enough for me to hear. I gave her fifteen and thanked her. She gave me the hint of a smile.

A big blond with huge breasts and a tiny waist came up to me and asked me how I was doing. She had a slightly raspy voice, cigarette breath that matched the place, and a white bikini. A bit of conversation.

"Yes, hunting."

"Congrats on your kill."

Small talk. A little bullshit.

I acted as I do with strangers sitting next to me on airplanes and said I was a surgeon. She had no choice but to believe me and she chewed strawberry gum, which wasn't strong enough to mask her breath. She squatted next to me and put a hand on my thigh to keep her balance. The message was clear. She told me the prices and I said that I would wait a while. She persisted for thirty seconds, moving her hand up the inside of my leg and pressing her breasts against my forearm. Then she stood up. I assumed that as in any business, there were quotas to fill. She was aggressive and most definitely wanted to make her money early in the evening so she could hightail it out of there. As she left, she ran her hand lightly across the back of my neck. She turned around, smiling too hard and moving off with a slow, old-fashioned and practiced sway of her hips. It was crude and dramatic but perfectly clear. Not exactly like the theatre.

I like understanding the codes: it makes me happy.

I was hard as a rock. Normally, that's enough. It's just that simple. I get an erection if there is desire and when there is desire, I want to make love. More than once, the girl has been beautiful and perfectly fuckable, but I didn't get hard. I need more. Men perpetuate the most dreadful falsehood when they lead women to believe that their erections are independent of their brains. There are no two things more closely linked in the entire universe. Even more so than day and night. I guess that laying the blame on my cock instead of on my morals is a lesser offense. Extenuating circumstances. But women get past it and for centuries, they have accepted plenty of infidelities on the basis of this simple lie. An erection requires desire. The truth is that men, in their deepest nature, can desire more than one woman at a time, and equally. That's the way it is. A man has to do battle with himself in order to guarantee a woman his exclusive loyalty. And it is precisely this violent strength that women want to be assured of when they demand fidelity. The strongest man is the one who knows enough to listen when he tells himself no. I like to understand the codes: it keeps me faithful. I downed the crème de menthe in one gulp and picked up my beer.

That was the first time since meeting Emma that I touched someone else's breasts. Or rather, that breasts touched me. The geopolitical map of all my beliefs and promises had been shaken by my intentions and desires. Human nature seemed sad to me and, once again, too polarized. Fuck Saint Augustine, the inventor of concupiscence. Sleeping with the dancer or a girl or anything else at all was out of the question. But I am exasperated by the consequence of a moral principle that I am attempting to master. There are evenings when men suffer from personality disorders.

Will a world with three of four equal poles ever exist? What role does dust really play? Why do I live in a universe that is using itself up? Food, housework, thirst? Why can't I complete two perfect actions at the same time? If I can imagine such a world, it certainly must exist somewhere. FUCK YOU. I don't want to believe that it doesn't.

"Well anyway, if you change your mind, my name is Katie," said the half-naked blond dancer. And she sashayed back to her seat at the bar to wait.

Not only did I not change my mind about that but I have a thousand other ideas that don't change. And those are the ones that worry me. I got up and left the place like a hero who got a reprieve. You would be proud of your man, Emma. I won the first round. My adversary was a dancer. For another guy, it's a girl at the office; for another, it's the waitress serving lunch; for yet another, it's his wife's best friend.

When I closed the door of my truck, it was like turning off the TV: a bizarre but precious silence. I started the motor and hit the CD play button before getting back on the road. Radiohead's *OK Computer* on a continuous loop: "Karma Police."

The singer's high-pitched voice repeated several times that he had lost himself. I took a detour from the O. It could also have been a distorted O. As if it had been written in total darkness.

ON THE FLY

An intersection. A pickup transporting a deer idles under a traffic light, which hangs from wires that sway in the wind. The truck's turn signal

indicates that it will turn left. The light is green. Yellow. Red. Green.
Yellow. Red. Green. Yellow. Red. The man behind the steering wheel
pulls a disc out of the CD player and inserts another one. A few min-
utes pass. The man gets out, draws a line in the dirt with his left foot.
He climbs back into his seat, closes the door and the pickup takes off
again.

I didn't finish the O. A sense of emptiness gave me the urge
to go home. Emptiness makes me guilty. Or is it the opposite?
I could always go back to it one day. I'll have a good reason.
You have to be flexible.

I left a mark on the ground; I could have left a dime like
a golfer marking the placement of his ball on the green. I put
in one of Leonard Cohen's "best of" CDs. Interlude. I will start
again from there. I want my own restaurant.

More importantly, I missed her. Early November.

When I got back from Maniwaki, Emma told me Pietro was dead. We had stayed in contact. His had been a constant if less frequent presence.

I would have wanted him to talk to me. To talk to him. To make him talk. I imagine all these things he might have said in his slow, deep voice.

He had left a long handwritten letter.

"Dear Marc,

I hope I'll have the strength to pull the trigger.

Life is a fiction in which not all of us are characters.

I've been told that life's only truth is found in details so simple they only appear in the last moments of our existence. The only time I will have experienced such bewilderment is when I struggled against my nature. Abstinence and faith. I am a descendant of the Tuscan condottieri, those mercenary soldiers from the Middle Ages who built their fortunes and their power on spoils amassed while serving whichever master offered the most. Imperfect loyalty. I tried to repair whole generations in one lifetime.

I wonder what will be revealed at the very moment when death becomes dominant and irreparable within me. To whom are we naturally loyal? By default.

To ourselves, to the person who shares our life, to our children, to a friend...

I hope that a buried memory will emerge. Of myself as a child, resting my head on the knees of my mother, old even then, as she rocks me under the Naples sun, heavy as gold, waiting for it to set and for me to sleep. Her fingers that trace the shape of my ears and temples. She strokes my neck, too. I can fall asleep.

I would hate to be disappointed by something insignificant. And still I have hope.

All these truths that we hide.

Giving blood is detrimental to the health of the donors but it's still less dangerous than being short of blood in a hospital. And all these wars, all these efforts to create death just because someone powerful thinks that they're serving the good of all mankind.

True evil is always isolated, out of synch with the self.

The most mortal of wounds have always been provoked by tacit and collective agreements. In 1870, Pius IX decreed papal infallibility. From then on, popes would always be right, no matter what they said. Go see what Pius XII had to say about the Holocaust."

I read Pietro's letter, knowing that I would read it only once. He continued.

"Life is a fiction in which human nature, unknowingly, plays its own role. At the end of a complete and lucid life – my own – I cannot come to any conclusions. I did not understand anything fundamental. Oh, I certainly and very dogmatically feigned the contrary with my deeds and acts and the identity that the Church robe gave me.

I gave sermons, some with conviction and others because people wanted to hear them. I was powerful because people believed me. Not vice versa. Like the mercenaries. Such gravity.

The verb 'to have to' and its implementation are an abomination. You'll have to, you must, we have to do it. That's where Satan is: we replace our volition with an obligation. You must sacrifice your lives, your generations. You have to be happy and that's an order."

Go on, Pietro, I am listening. I imagine the sounds that come from beyond the grave. I am sitting, alone at the table, but I hear you. Silence surrounds me. The world on MUTE, but I hear you.

I hear thinking. How is that possible? Centuries of progress. Millennia of spectacular advances. Our perception of speed is erroneous because although the speedometer reads three hundred kilometres per hour, we've forgotten that the scenery is moving at the same speed.

Emma seemed worried and asked me if everything was alright. "Yes...yes," I said aloud. I hadn't even taken off my hunting jacket.

I got caught up in humanity's most banal and predictable game. It would take the absence of a man for me to measure his importance. I hate that this man is summed up in a few hand-written pages. But there was still more.

"Five thousand years of recent history and still there are wars, famines, diseases and poverty. We are so slow. I was sure that death was a genetic mistake, that we would change the order of things and repair the affront. I was wrong.

Today, I am tired of living, tired the way you feel after staying up all night. I am sleep deprived. A degenerative disease is killing me now.

The sun came up, my reddened eyes burn and I want to sleep. I guess this is part of the modern quest to be happy. To find happiness through wealth, one's possessions, one's family, one's clothes, one's food, one's body, through one's beliefs. On the seventh day, he rested and aspired to happiness.

When the angels play for God, they play Bach, but when they play for themselves, they choose Mozart.

Even angels want to be happy. What a world!

Running after happiness has replaced the simplicity of contented solitude. And so the obsession of the West subtly spreads to Eastern religions. I don't know if we should leave things or ideas behind when we die. I know that in a restaurant, you leave a tip. Should I leave something for those who will follow?"

I'll miss you, Pietro. It would have been nice if you'd have gotten to know Emma. She's right here and she wants to comfort me, but I'm not sad. I'm happy to read you and hear you. What if God doesn't exist? In the future, it will be easier for me to believe that He does not exist than to believe that He does. I have alarm bells permanently ringing in my head. I will live in a deafening plenitude from now on.

Pietro spoke to me from farther and farther away. The seven pages of his letter weighed heavily in my hand. His voice grew weaker. It blended with those of Emma and Elmyna, asking why I wasn't answering. His words mingled with my thoughts. It occurred to me that I would have written the same thing in a suicide note.

One last page.

"I remember the chicken slaughter and I think that it could be the final image of my film, my life could end with that. On the wall of a lean-to behind the house, there were metal cones, hanging too high for a boy my age to reach. The chickens were slid down into them head first, and there they were caught, unable to struggle. My mother took the head, which hung out of the opening at the bottom of the cone, pulled the carotid artery away from the neck and made a small, silent slit with a knife. Without making a sound, the chickens stayed there, in a forced calm, and spilled their blood in great droplets, like rain falling when there is no wind. They kept their eyes open until the very last second when, miraculously, it seemed, because I had never seen them blink, their eyelids appeared. Dead. We, too, have eyelids. And God needs us as much as we need Him."

Emma and the little one left the room. I lay down on the sofa and a memory came back to me. I had once masturbated while thinking about the Virgin Mary, and finally about the statue of the Virgin Mary, which I found beautiful, the woman of all women. She was there in that life-sized plaster statue in the school chapel's basement. Left hand on her heart and the right, onto which I had ejaculated, open as if to beseech my soul. I was sixteen. And I could not get rid of this desire.

Taking a life is not a game, despite what some people think, but a very lucid moment when this certitude responsible for causing death is the only time when a true dialogue between man and his conscience occurs.

Working in a slaughterhouse has no connection to these physical efforts for reconciliation. Wanting to intentionally cause the death of a living being, apart from oneself, is as symbolic an act as making the sign of the cross. And this whole journey also served to postpone my own death. To subdue it. To dull its senses. Pietro's letter was a ringing bell. An Angelus.

Aspartame is a poison.

I imagine that at the end of a long, rich, intense and tranquil life, I will come to the conclusion that the human psyche has not budged for centuries. But maybe we should be content to remain at a standstill. Why always strive to move forward? The obsession with progress is emasculating. The spirit's impotence cannot be cured in a fertility clinic and Viagra can do nothing to help the erectile dysfunction of ideas.

I would have liked to write a play for you, Pietro, because when someone close to us dies, a void is created and we get carried away by excesses of great goodwill. I had found my title: *The Capons of Happiness.* The entire first act would have taken place in a confessional. And the rest, in Paradise.

Religions provide palliative care for humanity.

I have mourned my species and feel not the least bit of resentment. God did not create men as equals; instead men invented a god that, had he existed, would have made them so.

Why this shame, this refusal to take our lives for what they are? I am not talking about eliminating the spiritually impoverished, or doing away with the old and the ill, or making entire countries infertile and extinguishing peoples...quite the opposite. I mean accepting these differences and making sure there are less of them. Like an evangelization that would not serve the powerful. I become an optimist when I drink.

I developed a respect for my mother's indigenous race because it had a perpendicular function to the modern Western model. America belonged to that people. Truly. Before it became an ill-at-ease adolescent.

Wild birds never knew corn, as the proverb goes.

We were force-fed a god who is not ours.

Can the soul be like the liver of a force-fed duck?

This is how Pietro's letter ended:

"In the last seconds of my life, I would have liked you to teach me how to say that word for being in denial, so beautiful in your mother tongue, because it says more than all the sentences that try to explain it: *Kattonhiha.*"

I fell asleep. I hadn't cried. I threw the whole letter away. And Pietro would never speak to me again.

I am neither mercenary nor patriot. I have no specific leanings and no political ideologies. When I vote, I vote as often for the left as for the right. My morals are dying. Could someone inject me with Faith, Love, Hate or the idea of Happiness?

The only force that I recognize as having dominance over me is superstition. Not the superstition of heaven or sorcerers but the kind I can act upon, the kind that compels me to create our existence.

I could have invented you, Emma, had you not been there. Can a miracle exist without religion?

I am grateful to the Great Design for not making me a king, the commander of an army, a pope or the leader of a nation. Because then I would have played with the map of the world. I would have made a great dictator, with wars and alliances and millions of deaths. Just like that. Because of social will. Because of humanity. So that History will be a true story.

I preferred to escape.

I went back to sleep.

I did not mourn Pietro for very long. This doesn't worry me because time, like the wind, sands down all of the landscape's rough edges and finally softens even the sharpest pain. As it does for slaughtered animals.

The memory endures: it is a sharp-edged stele and the memories become the balm, just in case.

I am going to leave again. I know it.

I like running away. It's the only place from which I will not flee. Toward any destination, there is a path that I hasten to mark with a sense of urgency. We always run when we make an escape. This running allows me to keep moving forward. To not look back. This is a luxury, a privilege stolen from the memory of all those years, the ugliest and the most beautiful, that our brain's awareness records and imprints. Without our realizing it.

The good deeds like the bad, regardless of their morality. I flee like the smoke that escapes a cold but still smouldering log: leaving only a gaseous trace, the smoke, and a small pile of grey ash scarcely heavier than dust. I love you, Emma, but I do not know how to stop there. Is it just normal to be in love? Perhaps it's a fault that I cannot openly admit to you.

Words are also a quick escape toward an incarnation of truth.

I hate Pietro for having died. He has a head start that I haven't managed to accept. That's the regression theory.

Species survive and adapt, particularly the strongest, but the end result is always the same.

I had so hoped to love you without failing, Emma. But I know that I will fail. Will I ever be able to stop atoning? I kill because I'm obsessed with death in all its horrific beauty. And this love that I poach, will it ever be satisfied?

The restaurant opened only a few weeks after I returned from Maniwaki. It occupied a long narrow space, like a French bistro. No tablecloths, of course. Wooden tables and a kitchen that opened onto the dining room. The first meal prepared was baby Brussels sprouts, quickly deep-fried and seasoned with garlic, a hint of hot pepper and lots of mint leaves, which I normally try to avoid. This accompanied a dish of stewed deer tripe. Dom Pérignon 1996. Corked. Consumed in a half-and-half blend with Red Bull. For dessert: maple syrup Jell-O in the shape of a heart, and at its centre, a little heart of salted foie gras – little mouthfuls about the size of a one-dollar coin. On the menu, it was called *coeurs gras*, which roughly translates as heavy hearts.

Emma and I were solid. So I told myself every morning and several times throughout the day. A steely respect in which I detected the single flaw: that I was both the strongest and the weakest link. For her, for myself, for us. The Holy Spirit of deception. My love for her was mutable. Had I struggled, I would have sunk like a stone. I suspected my morals of crumbling like leaves on the ground. Of being porous and corroded. Of being humus.

I got up one morning, thinking that I would be able to pick everything up where I left off solely because of desire. For the self, for the other, for us. But I must have been contaminated by social desire. I raise the weapon, I take aim, and I see myself behind the crosshairs.

I was eleven years old the first time I picked up a Kleenex that had fallen next to waste basket. Normally, I would have left it on the floor. I was always making silent promises to this game of snot basketball.

If I make this basket, I'll be rich.

If I make this basket, Janicka, that pretty girl in my class, will kiss me.

If I make this basket, I'll get a Coleco game for my birthday.

If I make this basket, God will appear to me.

Naturally, when the wadded ball of cellulose and mucus fell short of the target, I had the right to start over, and the game became a series of two out of three or three out of five, until I finally won. I made hundreds of wishes each and every day, until my adolescence came to an end. Some of those wishes came true, while others did not, and eventually the game became no more than a reflection of my fear and my obligations. The human lottery of hope. The one that makes us hope; the one that assuages our deep disappointment.

I saw myself then as a stranger to the idea I had of myself. So I stopped retrieving the Kleenexes that missed their mark. Stopped retrieving my own unfulfilled wishes. Like kilometres of asphalt swallowed so as not to tell a soul. To hide billions of personal truths from billions of people. All those ideas that will not exist. Am I the only one in the universe who never stops thinking and yearning?

Who endures lucid anguish over everything and over nothing? Ceaselessly, except when I drink?

Some mornings, I am tired of being me. Especially this morning, in the car. I'd like to be someone else. Suffering someone else's anguish encourages me not to get upset about it.

Why do you love me, Emma?

I always think about the people who pick the fruit I eat. Five thousand kilometres south of me, a man, a woman, a child picked the banana I'm eating. The clementine in December. Did the Chinese Xuang Pei question the origin of the extract of black bear gallbladder that he's going to ingest in order to get a nice erection? We too easily forget that everything is connected: people come from other people and things come from other things.

Emma wanted another child. Like a request.

"I know my life isn't complete yet."

I envied her certainty. Like when I'm drunk and know tons of things. Or at least have fewer doubts.

"For the good of our species?" I thought. "Are you sure? Of me?" Women are the ones who have to perpetuate the race. They know.

She will decide. If we ever split up, it will have been her choice. There's the restaurant we just opened and the little girl we already have. And then there's this urge to reproduce. I share the woman I love with the invisible progress of the human race. And soon it won't be me sharing her with our children but our children who will accept, without too much complaint, that I still kiss her a few times a month.

To my great surprise, making a baby has become the ultimate fantasy. The biggest turn-on in the world. Worth a thousand bear gallbladders and tons of shark fin aphrodisiacs. FUCK the other species.

I understand the male deer. Ejaculating into a fertile woman is now as meaningful as going hunting. You can shoot at me, but let me live to reproduce another autumn. The fallout from your decision, too. Thank you, Emma, for that: no precautions, no worries, no insistence, no false pretenses. This woman wanted only that I come inside her. This desire. My erection could last a full one hundred years. I believe in desire.

From time to time, I thought about something else.

Did you know, Emma, that seven centuries after Jesus Christ, the Lateran Council decreed that the Virgin Mary was a virgin? Seven centuries after his death.

I finally feel useful. I exist because my obligation to the species has been fulfilled. And it's the most sexually stimulating thought there is. I even wondered if this was some kind of trap. Why does pleasure have to be associated with this act? Don't Hasidic men cover their women from head to toe with a white sheet, leaving only one opening for genital contact? Finished, she puts her wig back on and gives birth.

Are gays a superior race that would imitate the reproductive act without running the risk of overpopulation? The Earth is like an elevator: it has a maximum capacity that must not be exceeded.

Spelling mistake.

I like driving drunk. Staying the course like a ship's rudder. With some slack. Loud music. At night. Not during the day.

Pietro is dead. I answer to no one but you, sweet Emma. I did not sleep with the dancer. I desired her like thousands of others and I resist with all the strength of the Universe, if it exists. They say that since the Big Bang, the universe has been expanding. But into what? Into what space does it grow?

My universe is horizontal. A sinuous route that unfurls before me. The expansion is invisible to the naked eye without a telescope the size of a planet.

The restaurant is open. December 27th. Gifts, wishes, snow and my head still making the noises of a hungry belly. I went back to Maniwaki. The same emptiness that drove me back to Montreal at the end of October brings me back to this northern crossroads where I must complete my O. And vice versa. It's like faith, once again. You do it simply because you decided to believe.

Tsothohra. The time of cold. The month of December.

Failure is nothing but the poor synchronization of our deepest desires and reality itself. The explanation is required in America. Sometimes I wish I had Down's syndrome.

I headed toward Mont-Laurier. Don't ask questions. Over a deserted road, a flashing light dangled from four wires as if being held at a distance. We met at a similar intersection in

Michigan. Now I know what had made me so afraid two months ago. And I also know why I came back.

I continue. I turn left to finish the O. It's done. Maniwaki. I know. There were only a few metres left. I could easily have completed the circle the last time. But it's only projection into the future that truly keeps me alive. One thing to accomplish at a later date and my future is assured. My survival is achieved through these leaps into the future. An existential kangaroo. I stay alive because things are planned and scheduled. Projects are subpoenas. Seems to me I could have died, here at this crossroads, under the traffic lights, at the very same place where I had once used my left foot to draw the line where I would resume the letter O. The two months taken up with opening the restaurant and making a baby will have been nothing but the behind-the-scenes of a play. The making of another play. Now I only have to trace the U and I'll have said what I have to say to America.

Another urge. Another hesitation. I took the same break at the same intersection and played the same Leonard Cohen CD. I stopped at the same spot. I found my mark on the ground, under the snow. To the right, I return home; to the left, the dancer.

Cohen decided for me when he sang the last verse of "Democracy." Through the speakers, he told me that he's neither left nor right but just staying home in front of a hopeless little screen. I won't go left or right either; I'll go through this intersection heading north instead. Immobility must have killed so many people. I transcended the home-dancer polarization. In the rear-view mirror, I can see the smile on my face.

Parc de La Vérendrye. Then later to the west and finally to the north toward Val-d'Or. My great-grandfather had prospected for gold in Dawson. Always searching. I have come to the conclusion that finding is a drag. And it's almost always disappointing.

After four hours on the road, during which I had seen only three cars and a semi-trailer, I arrived in Amos at seven in the morning. I filled the gas tank and then took the 109 North toward Matagami. The road to James Bay starts there. Another kilometre zero.

I hope to grow old with you, Emma. I hope that we'll rock on the porch on Sundays, waiting for the children to come home and eat with us. The kitchen will smell of venison braised with thyme and savory. We'll tell each other that we have done well. The best we could.

In Matagami, I filled the tank again and wondered when the public health officials would tell us that high-frequency wavelengths are detrimental to our health. Televisions, telephones, radar equipment, satellites and other sources of electromagnetic waves are responsible for a cellular abnormality that causes cancer, among other things. BlackBerry tumour.

It is minus twenty-eight degrees Celsius on this late December morning. The sky is infinitely clear. Deep blue. There are only Cree Indians at the garage. When you take the road to James Bay, you have to register at the barrier and provide your contact information for security purposes.

"The next gas station is at kilometre 381," the clerk tells me. "Watch out for the caribou, too, some guys have seen them at about the 200 mark."

A million animals that start out from the sixtieth parallel and move down to the fifty-second to find food during the winter. Rebuilding their strength, going back up north and reproducing there once again.

"Thanks."

And I drove. Then I drove and then drove some more. Even when you've been driving for a long time, there's still ten times more to go. The road never ends. From time to time, a little post indicates the parallel: 52, 53, 54. The scale has changed. You no longer count kilometres, you note latitudes. I'm getting farther away from everything.

The highway goes on like this for 622 kilometres, all the way to Radisson. At kilometre 544, you can turn right. Euphoria. The Trans-Taiga Road. Another seven hundred kilometres from west to east, all the way to Caniapiscau. All the hydroelectric plants that supply the northeastern part of North America are found there: LG2, LG3, LG4, La Forge-1, La Forge-2, Brisay.

Ahead of me, the trees are disappearing. They grow smaller and smaller, more stunted. The hills flatten out, abraded by millions of years of arctic winds and glaciations. Thousands of utility poles stand between them like modern versions of Cervantes' windmills. At each curve, at every plateau, the infinite reappears. After a while, it gets even more infinite. The taiga gives way to the tundra, and bit by bit, the tundra turns into a feeling of love. Slow and extraordinary. Remote, harsh, unmoving and magnificent.

I don't think I met anyone but Cree. No Inuit. Too far south. They turn up around the fifty-fourth parallel, just after Radisson, where it stays dark later in the morning and gets dark earlier at the end of the day. I am alone. Leonard Cohen has been singing in a loop since I left Mont-Laurier. Janis Joplin gave him a blowjob in New York's Chelsea Hotel on 23rd while a limousine waited for him on the street below. The miracle is not the blowjob but the song that still lasts to this day.

I saw my first caribou at kilometre 220. You have to slow down because, surprise, they prefer running along the road to leaving it. Another world. These animals came down from the north in the biggest and longest wild migration of all the mammals. The Kurds migrated. So did the Jews, the West Africans... The Western white man of North America has not migrated for centuries. He found enough food, safety, comfort and women on this continent. He grew lazy. He discovered fried food. Twice a year, every year, the caribou cover a distance equal to the distance between Miami and Montreal. Marvellous prehistoric beasts. Independent and emancipated. Hundreds of thousands of them will never see a human being during their lifetime.

When I saw them, I had the urge for hot blood mixed with ground spruce needles. Thereby drinking and eating of the only life in the area. There's nothing here but spruce trees and snow. Sometimes caribou. The world is simple. The ground is white. The spruce are brown, almost black. The same colour as the Holy Tunic of Argenteuil.

Their flesh is rich in iron. Hepatic. Cree and Inuit women know nothing of anemia.

According to the law, I can hunt anywhere between kilometre 498 on the James Bay Road and Radisson, and on the Trans-Taiga Road.

I drove without interruption. The end has no end. I love you, Emma. My tundra. How can you switch between worlds without sleeping or marking the transition with a ritual like dreams, a kiss or the night? This interminable movement forward keeps taking me farther away from you and bringing me closer to myself. Is it possible that faith also migrates? I successfully moved from one world to another while keeping my head on straight. Except for the alcohol I drink to make the journey seem less long.

I stopped after kilometre 497, just before reaching kilometre 498. I waited with Mr. Cohen for a good hour. Three trucks with Cree on board drove past me, and at the very moment when Cohen began to sing "Hallelujah," a small herd of five caribou decided to cross the road. At that time of year, the males and females aren't living together anymore. Dead meat walking. They meet only to mate earlier in the fall. No shrinks, no lawyers and no guilt. The caribou are faring well. No shared custody. That's the difference between them and me. I wouldn't like to be away from Elmyna.

The migration to southern territory begins soon after mating. Mainly to find food, these animals will form groups of several hundreds and then travel thousands of kilometres. The colder it is earlier in the season, the sooner the migration gets underway because caribou use the frozen lakes to reach their winter feeding grounds in the south. A south that is still far to the north of us.

Their hooves are like giant upside-down soup spoons, curved inward, concave, thus giving them more support on the snow while still allowing them to scrape it away to uncover the precious lichen that provides the energy necessary for their survival. Caribou: the one that paws the earth to find food.

There was a little fawn in the group of five. Meaning they were all females, since the Grand Order had granted them the inalienable right to care for the species' offspring.

They stayed ten long minutes licking at the last metres of the roadside at kilometre 497, looking for the calcium chloride that is mixed with sand and spread in great quantities to melt the snow and ice. I got out of the pickup; I loaded my rifle. And I aimed at the biggest female in the group. I saw the green and white notice in my telescopic sight, a kilometre away, announcing the start of the legal hunting zone. The caribou were standing somewhere between me and the sign.

For some strange reason, you always look for the biggest animal. When our children are born, the only significant reference point is still the baby's weight: six pounds three ounces, seven pounds eight, eight and four. The same goes for hunting. A buck weighing 240 pounds. A moose weighing 720 pounds, a female caribou weighing 175 pounds. It's only with adults that this doesn't fly. A 230 pound woman is not exactly a prize.

I loaded two cartridges into the rifle. My heart was beating fast and strong. Like when we kissed for the very first time. I took aim.

Return.

The clerk at the registration station in Matagami asked me if I had killed any caribou. "No," I answered as I fiddled with the two unused cartridges in the right-hand pocket of my coat. I hadn't fired the gun.

The road is like a scrapbook full of memories.

The first time we kissed, early in the morning, in Toronto, after having told me in Mohawk that she was tired, she said, "I like the softness of silk." I don't know why. Lots of sentences like that that didn't need to go any further.

I replied, "Between the months of June and August of 1989, I only watched TV with my head upside down." She said nothing more. I told her that the Sudarium of Oviedo, in Spain, was a piece of cloth that had been wrapped around Christ's head when his body came down from the cross. She shook her head. I still don't know why.

We were not smiling when we kissed a second time. And we fell asleep without going any further.

I had not fired on the caribou because I could not. There they were, a hundred feet away from of me. Unmoving pale grey targets. Looking a bit stupid, they gazed at me. My finger on the trigger. In my sight, I saw the gleam of the guard hairs that keep them warm. A soft steam rose off my hands and up toward the sky. The soft steam that rose from their nostrils showed me their exhalations. Every sound was amplified. The snow was blue; the weather, dry. It was twenty-five degrees below, but nervousness made me forget the cold. I no longer heard Leonard Cohen, who was still singing his intelligent words about love. That was when I first realized I wasn't jealous of him anymore. I lowered my rifle. The caribou seemed smaller but also more alive. Life goes on. They know nothing. I envy them. They are almost dead. They just don't know it. Failed lives.

I often imagine myself in the place of these animals that I kill.

What would I know? That another species had killed me? That this dry, deafening noise is the end? That this burning in my body will put me to sleep? Does it hurt? Or does the intensity of the moment relegate the pain to the background? Is it better not to know that a bullet to the brain turns out all the lights? Is it really a surplus value to die suddenly without suffering? Unaware of what has happened?

Can we give ourselves absolution?

I climbed back into the pickup to turn around. Through the noise my feet were making, which was like the sound of Corn Flakes being crushed against an arctic snow, I heard Leonard singing something about philosophy and Johnnie Walker.

I hit the replay button.

When I've been drinking, I sing and I believe the words that I hear. It makes me more amorous. As if it was me saying them.

I would have liked to make a dish of tripe and chorizo with caribou stomachs and a Spanish pepper, as I had when the restaurant opened. I would have liked to stuff the second stomach with oysters, eat the tongue as sashimi, make a spruce-needle blood pudding. Eat the eyes like candy, like Inuit children.

Instead I ate a bag of Doritos that was lying around in the truck.

I left the tundra and returned to the taiga. Then to the boreal forest. Fifteen hours of driving. At Mont-Laurier, I took the Maniwaki to Pembroke route, toward Ontario, and then went on to Bancroft. I crossed Lake Ontario on an eight-berth ferry at Cobourg and arrived in Rochester, New York without ever seeing a customs inspector. A little farther to the south, toward Ithaca. There's a brand of firearm bearing this name. Cooperstown – Albany – Saratoga Springs. Mohawk country.

For years people believed that Mohawk Indians were cannibals who ate their enemies. Mohawk means "those who eat animate things." Like me. The land of my mother's forefathers had no borders. South of the Hudson and north to the Saint Lawrence in Montreal.

And the rest of Interstate 87 in the Appalachians, up to the Canadian border at Saint-Bernard-de-Lacolle, Quebec.

"Where do you live? How long have you been gone? Did you buy or are you bringing back anything other than your personal effects?"

"Montreal...ten days...no..."

"The purpose of your trip?"

I'm going to have to lie to you. It's for your own good. I took a sidelong glance at the passenger seat next to me where I had left the map of the United States with FUCK YOU written on it. I would have liked to explain everything to him – and to you, too, Emma – beginning with the incident with Denise at CEGEP. Then again, maybe not. I love crossing borders. The adrenaline rush.

The truth is not made for you, anonymous keeper of false, geographic borders. Would you know what to do with it? No one forces us to be honest. You are not qualified to hear it. You were trained to be suspicious and to sniff out lies. Not to check the spelling of a guy who used his pickup truck to write FUCK YOU across the page of a continent.

One thousand and ninety-two kilometres. Back in Montreal.

I am not indispensable to the functioning of others. Things continue their back and forth in an imperceptible movement regulated by something far greater and stronger than myself. Sometimes, absence is a regulator. *Rahtentyes*. To leave.

One day, apropos of life, mine in particular: "Ah! So that's all it was."

I don't want that to be all it is. I don't want to understand and reduce. I hate retrospectives: they fill in the time with white walls.

I would also like to understand the framework of the space that we occupy on a moral level.

I miss Pietro. I will not be infallible but I can act before making a mistake. Choose the lesser of two disappointments. At this rate, I won't make it past the age of thirty-five. I know how to kill live animals.

Disappointment is a deadline that I try to postpone.

ON THE FLY
A man gets out of a pickup truck. He walks slowly, as if in a daze, and enters a house, a sack on his back and a box in his hands. He stores his gun in a locked cupboard and slowly takes out another box and another gun, which he sets aside. He locks the cupboard and goes to the fridge, to which is taped a post card of a painting illustrating a descent from the cross. He opens the door and when he closes it, there are black shapes in one hand. A woman and a little girl sleep upstairs.

When I got back to the house, I ate three big, fresh black truffles. Raw. I will crap that smell for two days straight. That wasn't part of the plan.

There are more and more days during the year when I am able to say that I love her. Saying it is like pulling the trigger of a gun. This love judges and sentences me to a bitter disappointment. Intolerable, vile and worst of all. Not to disappoint Emma.

I love her when she puts her hair up and sighs in exasperation in front of the mirror each morning. When she counts her wrinkles and looks for new ones. When she asks me if I still love her and why. And that my answers are always insignificant. I love when she nudges me with her nose so that our mouths touch.

I adore it when she turns a bit to the side to check her profile in the mirror and stands on tiptoe for a better view of her behind.

I am amazed that I'm still in love. I love you. I have to learn how to produce this sound.

In 1983, a study out of California's Stanford University proved beyond the shadow of a doubt that sexual activity reduces aggression and violence in men. There is also sufficient evidence to prove that hormones are responsible for wars and revolutions and that they are the basis of all religions. Especially in the month of May.

Inside me, a system operates without my knowledge. I now know that it is not spiritual.

December 29th.

I always loved to come back home. It was snowing in Montreal.

As I put the rifle back in the cupboard and took my gun out of its case, I thought of the first time Emma and I made love. I remember my eagerness to be inside her. And then it happened without any pressure, all our desires in tune. I found I was inside her, and thinking back on it now, I know that this is the first true Faith I decided to have. Driven by an absolute. I will not be a pope, but I will believe in myself just as strongly. Without cynicism.

The only belief for which I am entirely responsible: my belief in the imperative of the flesh. The one that compels the survival of my species but is also connected to pleasure, like a computer chip, a precaution, considering the deterioration of our condition.

I suspect the Grand Order of having associated pleasure with our reproductive process as a safety measure, to ensure our survival. Just in case we all would have wanted to become abstinent popes. And all these things that are not me, that are not us. Migratory birds are faithful; mammals like me are not. The females of my species require me to be so and I acquiesce. It's us against Nature. To arms, citizens!

I love her when she blinks her eyes, when she takes off her shoes at night after spending a day on her feet. I love when she concentrates on putting colour on her lips, eyelashes and eyelids. When she rocks herself, alone in silence. When she absentmindedly plays with her earring and when she closes her eyes in the bath. When she puts on lotion. Or when she looks at me and thinks I don't see her.

I tried to reconcile my desires and my self-imposed commands. To make them mesh with hers.

How do we avoid being cynical? The delegated authorities of the UN declare a ceasefire in the Middle East and that is enough to heal real wounds, give respite and save real lives. Power has no daily life. The greatest good for the greatest number of people is but an illusion. The shepherd always leads his sheep for his own benefit, even if it's to slaughter.

So few have escaped this during the twentieth century.

I loaded two cartridges into the gun, although obviously one would suffice. And I wanted to pull the trigger, but I passed out instead.

I opened my eyes and saw the ceiling. I heard noises outside. On the TV, a video of Oasis was playing. Passersby and cars outside. As usual.

I didn't unpack my bag of clothes; I left it in the front hall. I put the gun back in the cupboard. I will die some other time. Maybe tomorrow. I went upstairs after the newscast on which they would not announce my death. I wanted to sleep, as usual. I will finish the U of my FUCK YOU some other morning. I kissed her neck.

ON THE FLY
A woman, in a bed, turns toward a man, kisses him deeply and whispers something in his ear.

Later.

Stretched out on the dry leaves of another autumn, I wait for my prey.

There are noises in the forest. The gun is resting on my chest. I feel its weight as it rises and falls with my respiration. I am finishing the U. I look at the sky. A buzzard flies overhead. It sees and surely recognizes this murmuring.

I watch the planes that are everywhere now. Flight paths are rectilinear graffiti: boring and invisible, they transport hundreds of humans. Even thousands of kilometres from all civilization, there is air traffic. I could have started my U on Bylot Island in Nunavut, no more and no less than the ends of the earth, where idiotic rich tourists from Asia, sitting in a plane, would have passed only ten kilometres above me while I would have spent thirty hours in a car and eight in a bush plane to get away from epicentres. Real distance is horizontal. Between us. On a sofa.

The North and South Poles, even Cape Horn, have become cruise ship destinations. Vanity tourism now draws visitors to Sir Shackleton's South Pole. There is nothing truly authentic left, save for the latitude of the caribou, wedged between a romantic North Pole and the asphalted sham called America.

The buzzard is a protected species. Majestic. Hunting it prohibited since time immemorial. I baited it with dead rabbits. When night falls, the bird will be more trusting.

Did you know, Emma, that a ring around the moon at night means rain the next day?

I am lying motionless on the ground, which is slowly decomposing. I no longer hear my breathing, just this voice inside me. Like being buried alive in a coffin, six feet underground, perhaps.

There is nothing but the expectation of death, and this thought that goes tic-tac, calming my spirit. And this bird that soars.

Born in 1970, Marc Séguin divides his time between his home in Montreal and his Brooklyn, New York, studio. He has exhibited his art (the cover of *Poacher's Faith* is his work) at the most prestigious contemporary exhibitions and fairs, including those held in Venice, Basel, New York and Miami. *Poacher's Faith* is his first novel.